MW01087532

The Ultimate
Treasure

MELODY
ANNE

The Ultimate Treasure

The Lost Andersons: Book Five

Copyright © 2016 Melody Anne

All rights reserved. Except for use in any review, the reproduction or utilization of this work in whole or in part in any form by any electronic, mechanical or other means, now known or hereafter invented, including xerography, photocopying and recording, or in any information storage or retrieval system, is forbidden without the written permission of the author.

This is a work of fiction. Names, characters, places and incidents are either the product of the author's imagination or are used fictitiously, and any resemblance to actual persons, living or dead, business establishments, events or locales is entirely coincidental.

ISBN-13: 978-0692802618
ISBN-10: 0692802614

Cover Art by Adam
Edited by Karen Lawson
Interior Design by Adam

www.melodyanne.com
Email: info@melodyanne.com

 /MelodyAnneAuthor    @AuthMelodyAnne

First Edition
Printed in the USA

OTHER BOOKS BY MELODY ANNE

Billionaire Bachelors:
*The Billionaire Wins the Game
*The Billionaire's Dance
*The Billionaire Falls
*The Billionaire's Marriage Proposal
*Blackmailing the Billionaire
*Run Away Heiress
*The Billionaire's Final Stand

The Lost Andersons:
*Unexpected Treasure
*Hidden Treasure
*Holiday Treasure
*Priceless Treasure
*The Ultimate Treasure

Baby for the Billionaire:
*The Tycoon's Revenge
*The Tycoon's Vacation
*The Tycoon's Proposal
*The Tycoon's Secret
*The Lost Tycoon

Surrender:
*Surrender - Book One
*Submit - Book Two
*Seduced - Book Three
*Scorched - Book Four

Forbidden Series:
*Bound -Book One
*Broken - Book Two
*Betrayed - Book Three
*Burned - Book Four

Unexpected Heroes:
*Her Unexpected Hero
*Who I am With You - Novella
*Her Hometown Hero
*Following Her - Novella
*Her Forever Hero
*Her Accidental Hero - **Coming Soon**

*Safe in His Arms - Novella - Baby, It's Cold Outside Anthology

The Billionaire Aviators:
*Turbulent Intentions
*Turbulent Desires

The Midnight Series:
*Midnight Fire
*Midnight Moon
*Midnight Storm
*Midnight Eclipse

Becoming Elena:
*Stolen Innocence
*Forever Lost
*New Desires

Collaborations:
*Taken by a Trillionaire
*Fall into Love
*7 Brides for 7 Brothers

Novels:
*Finding Forever

PROLOGUE

L ANCE STORM SAT warily in a large armchair in a massive office feeling like a bug being analyzed while his father, Richard Storm, and his uncles, Joseph and George Anderson, sat before him, a look in their eyes not to be trusted.

"What do you think, boy?" Joseph asked, his voice thundering through the room.

Lance took another drink of his fine glass of Scotch as the words his family had been speaking for the past hour filtered through his brain. He wanted to agree with the men, but he knew there was a catch. When it came to his father and uncles there was always a catch. But, at this particular moment, they were holding the bait he so desperately wanted a large bite of.

Still, he sat silently, wondering if he had the strength to turn them down. By giving in to what they wanted, he was playing right into their hands. It was a difficult decision for him to make.

"We aren't growing any younger," George said, a frown appearing between his brows.

"I don't understand why you want this. What's in it for you?" Lance finally asked.

"We care about our family. We just want to help you *and* help Lexie," Richard said.

"How is this helping me?" Lance asked.

All three men gazed at him with innocent expressions he didn't at all trust.

"You've been lost. This will mean as much for you as it does for Lexie," Joseph told him.

Lance really couldn't think of a negative to the plan the old men had come up with. Then again, he'd never been one to back down when he was afraid. If anything, that only made him push that much harder.

"Let's do it," he said. He leaned back and grinned. The old men might have thought they'd gotten exactly what they wanted, but Lance would make sure he was the one who came out the victor.

CHAPTER ONE

THE MUSIC PULSED through the room, the lights were muted, and bodies merged as Alexa Mills closed her eyes and let the beat take her away. It might have been minutes, or possibly hours, but soon she was bumped in the arm, and her sister, Savvy, was smiling at her before tugging on her hand to lead her to the quieter alcove where they had a table waiting and they could actually speak without shouting.

"When you decide to unwind, Lexie, you really let it all go," Savvy said with a grin as she took a long pull of her water. Her sister's skin was gleaming. Lexie wasn't sure if her own flesh was covered in red spots or not. She was burning up from dancing for so long.

"This is my last night in the States with my favorite sister. I wanted it to be fun so you won't forget me," Lexie told her.

"You're only going to be gone for a month. You promised," Savvy said in a threatening way. "I will come and get you if you try to extend it any longer than that."

"I can't miss too much time away from my beautiful niece," Lexie assured her.

"Good. 'Cause she might find another favorite auntie if you do," Savvy teased.

"Ugh, since you and Ashton have gotten married you have become far too domesticated. You should be envious of this great adventure I'm going on, not sad that I won't be stoking the home fires," Lexie told her sister.

Savannah had spent a summer working for Ashton Storm, and the two of them might have had a bit of a rocky start, especially considering he'd had a fiancée when her sister had met him, but their love couldn't be denied. They were perfect together — almost too perfect, actually. As much as Lexie was happy for her sister's happiness, she had to admit, at least on some level, she felt a slight twinge of jealousy too.

Lexie assured herself she was too young, at twenty-seven, to be thinking those thoughts. She had plenty of time to live her adventures and see the world before she settled down. That was, *if* she settled down. Her father hadn't been the best example of a loving man. She didn't want to end up with someone like him, someone who would suck the life out of her instead of giving her wings to fly.

Now, she'd been funded to go to the Philippines to help children still suffering from a deadly typhoon several years ago. She wanted to go around the world and make a difference one step at a time. The grant she'd been given was a once-in-a-lifetime opportunity, and she wasn't giving it up for anything.

Even as a child, Lexie had known she wanted to make something more of her life and that meant helping others. She'd been abused by her father and abandoned by her mother, and she'd always had to lean heavily on her sister. She wanted to pay her sister's love forward. Savvy had sacrificed so much so Lexie could have as normal of a childhood as possible. Now, more than ever, Lexie was determined to help other youth.

"I'm really going to miss you, Sis. We've never been this far apart, and I've always protected you. It's hard for me to let go, even though I know you're perfectly capable of taking care of yourself," Savvy told her.

"I know you love me. That's what has made a difference in my life. I want to give back," Lexie assured her.

"I'm so proud of you. However, I want you to send me pictures every single day and check in with me so I won't worry," Savvy insisted.

"I will check in as much as I possibly can," Lexie told her.

Good. I still find it difficult remembering you're an adult who is more than capable of taking care of yourself."

"And that's why I love you so very much," Lexie said with a laugh. "I adore you."

"I know. It's mutual," Savvy assured her.

The night flew by too quickly, and soon Lexie was holding her sister extra tight as they said their goodbyes. Then she was off for the airport in the car her sponsoring company had sent. Her heart pounded as they turned off the freeway to the airport. It was going to happen. She was on her way to save the world.

Okay, she might not be saving the world on this particular trip, but it was a good start. Humanitarianism began one person at a time, she told herself.

When the car bypassed the main terminal, Lexie grew a bit nervous. She hadn't checked the credentials of the driver. What if he wasn't who he said he was? Her heart thudded, but she tried to remain calm.

"Where are we going?" she asked.

"Your flight is out of the private terminal," the driver assured her.

Lexie knew this was a legit company. She'd sat before them as she'd explained what she wanted to do, and nothing had seemed out of place. The paperwork she'd completed had been insane, but there was nothing wrong with it.

The car stopped at the private terminal, and she let out a breath of relief. The driver came around and opened her door before she had her seat belt off. He gave her a reassuring smile before offering her his hand.

Lexie had never used the private terminal before. This trip was already starting off with a bang — that was for sure. She stood beside the car and gazed around as the driver removed her two bags, and then she walked by his side as they entered the terminal.

Only a few people were milling around the beautiful building as the driver made his way to the back doors. Where was the TSA? The lines? The annoyance of a large airport? She had no idea, but she shouldn't be complaining — even internally.

They went through the back doors where a large jet was sitting on the tarmac. A man smiled as he spotted them then ran up and took her bags, leading them to the back where a machine was loading many boxes of what looked like supplies.

"I'm going in this?" she asked, stopping in her tracks as she looked at the sleek white jet with blue stripes running down it.

"This is your ride," the driver said as he tried to get her to move again.

"Are you sure? I'm Alexa Mills," she said, wanting to make sure he had the right person. This jet looked as if it belonged to some billionaire CEO, not to a non-profit company intent on saving the world.

"Yes, Ms. Mills, I'm sure," he said with a laugh. He finally got her to move forward. Lexie felt as if she were entering another universe. She expected to be wedged between two stout people in the back of a regular plane, not sitting luxuriously in a corporate jet.

Why she was worried, she wasn't sure. Maybe it was because she was going to serve those who were less fortunate than most. She felt slightly guilty traveling in style.

Without further arguing, Lexie stepped toward the jet. This was an adventure she'd been looking forward to for a very long time. She wasn't going to turn away now.

Stepping through the open door, Lexie felt her breath leave her. The pilot stood to the side with a greeting that she was unable to respond to, because she was looking around in total awe.

The interior was done in beige and black with sleek leather furniture and what appeared to be mahogany cabinets. Brass and crystal accents ran throughout the large space and the cream colored carpet was plusher than any other she'd ever seen.

This wasn't an unfamiliar world, and she still wasn't sure she was on the right jet. She was about to ask as her head swiveled back around to look at the pilot.

"Have a seat, Ms. Mills. We'll be ready for takeoff in a few minutes," he told her as he held out his hand.

"Where should I sit?" she asked, grateful her voice had returned.

"Anywhere you choose."

Lexie stepped forward and sat in one of the oversized chairs, sighing in pleasure at the way she sunk into it. Her fingers trembled as she reached for the seat belt. A young man in a smart suit came out and asked what she'd like to drink, and Lexie decided she needed some liquid courage. She ordered a vodka tonic and was happy when he returned quickly with her drink and a bowl of trail mix.

Soon, the door was shut. She heard the engines throttle up, and then the jet was taxiing down the tarmac. The captain announced for all to be seated, that they were third in line for take-off.

That's when the air shifted. Without turning around, she felt the oxygen in the large cabin begin to diminish. She sucked in a breath, and the intoxicating scent she knew only too well, infused her insides.

"Glad you made it, Lexie."

The deep, sexy voice sent a shiver through Lexie's body. Finally, she was able to command her head to turn as Lance Storm took the seat next to her, a confident smile on his lips.

"What are you doing here?" she asked.

"I'm your benefactor for this trip," he told her with a twinkle in his eyes.

Lexie's stomach dropped. What in the world had she just gotten herself into?

CHAPTER TWO

L ANCE HAD KNOWN from the moment his father and uncles had come up with this plan for his company to sponsor Lexie on her save-the-world mission that he'd accompany her. He and Lexie had enjoyed one incredible night together at his brother's wedding, and then she'd avoided him like the plague from that moment on. A year later he still wanted to get her attention.

Now he definitely had it. They would be together in a foreign country for an entire month, enough time to either make her fall in love with him or get her out of his system. He wasn't sure which way he wanted it to go. But he knew beyond a doubt that if he had told her it was his company sponsoring the trip, she would have declined. And that would've foiled his plans.

Lance wasn't sure why she was running from him. The two of them had unbelievable chemistry. It wasn't that Lance was looking to marry or anything. He was the last holdout in his family. The rest of his siblings had taken their father's ultimatums and now seemed happy — happier than was normal, in his humble opinion.

He was glad for them, but it didn't mean he had to follow in their footsteps. On the other hand, he wasn't getting any younger. The days of living wild and free weren't as appealing as they once had been. Thus, he found himself chasing after a woman he wasn't sure wanted to be caught.

Wasn't that part of the fun though? Lance was wealthy, good-looking, and had a hell of a family. He could have his pick of women, but the one he wanted most was his sister-in-law's little sis. It might not be the best idea to keep chasing her; he could think that all he wanted, but his course of action had been full-on pursuit.

Lexie was gazing at him like he was an apparition as the plane lifted into the air. He wanted to reach out and touch her, assure her he was one hundred percent real, but he also enjoyed the shock on her face.

"What do you mean, you're my benefactor?" she asked him after several silent moments.

"My company picked you for this project," he told her as he lifted his Scotch and took an enjoyable sip. "You were recommended by some very reliable sources." He wasn't telling her they happened to be his father and uncles.

Lexie ran her fingertip over her frosted glass before lifting it to her luscious pink lips, downing at least half of it in a single gulp. She was nervous and anxious, but he wasn't sure if it was the surprise of him being there or simply because he made her antsy. He knew she wasn't frightened of him, maybe of what they'd had together, but most certainly not of him. They'd been great together the night of his brother's wedding, and he hadn't been able to forget about her since.

As a matter of fact, that might be half his problem. He hadn't bedded another woman since that night three hundred seventy-six days ago. His pants tightened thinking about it. He desperately hoped being locked together in a foreign country for the next thirty days would make her just as desperate for him as he was for her.

"Is this a joke, Lance?" she asked, her eyes narrowing.

The flight attendant came and offered them a refill. Lexie accepted and the man disappeared quickly but returned to tell them dinner would be served in twenty minutes. Lexie gave him a semblance of a smile and Lance nodded as the attendant retreated again to give them some much-needed privacy.

"Not at all. My company has been in the Philippines since the typhoon hit, rebuilding and bringing supplies. For this mission, we'll be there for a month, teaching preparedness and bringing progress to the area."

"We?" she asked with a squeak before clearing her throat and taking another big drink from her glass. "You're going to be there the *entire* time?" Lance wasn't sure if he should be offended or not by the panic in her eyes.

"Yes, I like to go over and help," he told her. Sure he hadn't stayed for a full month before, but then he'd never had such appealing company with him either.

"I would think you have much more important things to do," she told him.

Lance chuckled. "I buy and sell businesses, Lexie. I can do that from anywhere. I'm all yours for the next thirty days," he said. His pants tightened even more. He was hers in more ways than one. She only had to accept what he was offering.

Lexie turned and looked out the window as the ground appeared farther and farther away. It was mid-November and many people had Christmas lights twinkling from their houses and fences, but they could no longer see them.

Lance hadn't always been a big fan of the holidays but as his family had grown over the past five years, he'd started to appreciate it all a bit more. He was a little bummed to be missing a huge Thanksgiving spread where his siblings and cousins all came together with their kids. The chaos was great, in his opinion, which was something he never would have thought he'd enjoy. But he didn't appreciate a quiet house now nearly as much as he once had.

Maybe he was getting old. At thirty-six, he shouldn't be thinking that way. He had many years left to worry about the future, he assured himself. But the more he thought about Lexie, the more he felt his future wasn't such a bad thing. Maybe he just needed to let go of what he had once thought was important and embrace a new journey.

He had never thought about a woman a year after he'd slept with her. But he still dreamed of Alexa Mills. He still woke up in a cold sweat because his dreams were so vivid he expected to reach out for her and finish what his dream had started.

There was a bedroom on his corporate jet. Maybe the two of them could make good use of it. The flight to the Philippines was long, and there wasn't much to do after they had dinner.

"Lexie . . ." Lance began to say. She lifted her arm to motion as she often did when talking, and Lance got an icy cold bath as she knocked his drink right into his lap. Her eyes widened in horror as he sucked in his breath, unable to utter any sound other than a gurgle. She'd efficiently taken care of the pulsing in his pants as ice coated an area frozen cubes should never be allowed to touch.

Jumping from his seat, Lance brushed off the flight attendant who hurried to come over and help. At the same time, Lexie reached into her bag and came out with a handful of napkins.

"I'm so sorry," she spluttered as she reached for him. Lance instantly hardened again as her hands came toward him. As much as he wanted her touching him there, she wasn't doing it for the right reasons, and he feared the second her fingers landed on him, innocent or not, he was going to turn into a caveman and throw her over his shoulder to show her that bedroom he'd just been thinking about.

"I might have needed a cooling off," Lance told her, his gaze burning into hers. She gasped and he had no doubt she'd gotten what he'd been saying because her eyes strayed down to his wet pants before flicking back up to his eyes.

Leaning over her, he enjoyed the desire he saw flicker into her eyes. He could kiss her right then and there, and she wouldn't fight him. But she'd find an excuse later and accuse him of violating her. They had a month together without interruption. He had to be smart about this.

"I'd better go change," he regretfully told her.

"You have clothes in here?" she asked. He was happy to see what appeared to be regret in her eyes when he pulled away.

"We're leaving for a month. Of course I have extra clothes," he told her with a chuckle.

She glared at him. "I know you have extra clothes, I just meant that mine are packed in a bag below," she said.

"I keep extras inside. I travel often," he told her. Then he turned and left, making his way to his empty bedroom. His gaze strayed to the bed and an instant image of the two of them entwined on top of the covers, their bodies sweating, their cries merging, had him so hard he was barely able to get his pants off.

This was going to be a long flight.

CHAPTER THREE

L EXIE DIDN'T LET out a breath of air until she heard the soft click of a door close after Lance disappeared down the hallway of the jet. How big was this plane? She was incredibly curious, but not enough to follow him. Not that the thought of doing so was completely abhorrent.

She sat in her plush chair, sipping on her newly refreshed drink, feeling a buzz roll through her system as she imagined him sliding those wet slacks down his muscled thighs, then hooking his thumbs into the tight waistband of his underwear and peeling them down his legs. She remembered those legs. She remembered well what was at the junction of them.

Closing her eyes, she thought about that magical night after her sister's wedding. Lance had been so handsome in his dark suit, his bright eyes gleaming, that flirtatious mouth smiling — and she'd fallen hard for his charm. It hadn't even taken alcohol to influence her. She'd had a little at the wedding, but she'd been fully aware of her decision to accompany him to his room.

She couldn't regret their night together. It had been unbelievable. She'd lost count of how many times the man had made her come with his thick package, his unbelievably magic fingers, and that divine mouth of his. He'd touched every square inch of her body, and when they'd both been too exhausted to do it one more time, she'd fallen into a dreamless sleep in his arms.

She'd woken in the early morning hours, her body tangled in his, her heart immediately racing. She'd barely been able to see the outline of his face, of his relaxed lips that almost appeared to be in a smile, but the thump in her heart at being there with him had scared her.

Her father had been a violent man, abusive and domineering. She'd promised herself she'd never get trapped into marriage, and one night with Lance had made her hear wedding bells in her head. She was sure it hadn't helped that she'd had the best sexual night of her life right after a beautiful wedding where her sister had made an exquisite bride, but it had scared her enough to untangle herself, grab her clothes, and sneak off before the sun rose in the sky. She'd then had to do the walk of shame through the posh hotel.

She'd seen Lance several times after that night, but she'd kept herself aloof, telling him nothing could come of the two of them. It was easier to stay with her convictions when she wasn't miles high in the sky, getting ready to fly to a foreign country away from her sister and her friends. What was she going to do if he put on his full charm? She wasn't sure she could resist him, because she wanted him just as badly as he appeared to want her.

Lexie tried to fill her mind with the dozens of women she was sure he'd been with after her. That thought only made her achingly jealous and made her want to stake her claim. But she didn't have a claim on Lance. He wasn't hers, and she certainly wasn't his. Even if they were going to be working on this project together, they wouldn't be with each other night and day. They'd be busy and exhausted, and she was sure she'd hardly see him. That would make it so much easier. She just had to survive this plane ride and then she'd be back to her normal self.

Lexie didn't hear the bedroom door open or close, didn't hear Lance's footsteps approach, but she felt him in the room with her again, felt that tug that ran through her entire system seconds before he sat down next to her. She couldn't help but look over at him.

Lance was spectacularly stunning when wearing a suit and tie, but in a pair of old college sweats and a tight T-shirt, the man had her panting. She lifted her drink to gain more liquid courage only to find it empty. It was as if the flight attendant was on call, because he was there offering her a fresh glass before she managed to set her empty one down.

She should tell the attendant she'd had enough, but she had a feeling the entire bottle couldn't calm her as long as she was in the same vicinity as Lance. She couldn't make eye contact with him anymore. She feared she'd do something stupid like jump from her seat and straddle him if she did, so instead, she focused on the little side table next to her as her fingernails drummed the smooth surface.

"I made sure to have some comfortable clothes brought in for you since we have such a long flight," Lance said, his voice startling her out of her thoughts.

"How did you know what size?" she asked, then felt her cheeks heat as she met his gaze and his eyes traveled over her form.

"I'd say I'm pretty familiar with your body," he told her with a wink.

Her heated flesh became uncomfortably hot, and she wished for a fan to cool herself. He *had* touched every inch of her with his fingers and mouth, but it had been over a year since that night. He had surely forgotten by now. The look in his eyes told her he hadn't.

"Thank you. That was considerate," she said, hating the breathless sound to her voice.

Thankfully they were interrupted as delicious salads were set before them. The flight attendant told them their main course would be out soon.

Lexie dove into her food like it was a lifeline and had a stilted conversation with Lance, who didn't seem to notice her increasingly stressed mood. She'd been so excited to go on this adventure and now she wasn't sure she'd last a day, let alone a month. She had to keep reminding herself that once they were on the ground, she'd be free of Lance.

But the thought of being so close to him, but not close enough, was almost more torture than she could handle. She really needed to make up her mind. She'd only been with two men in her life, and that included Lance. It wasn't as if she had a ton of sexual experience, but she almost wished she could be that girl who had a tawdry affair without it affecting her emotionally.

Sex was soothing for the soul, wasn't it? Maybe if she could convince herself that it wouldn't be as emotional for her as it had been the last time, she could undo her pants and feel the magic only Lance could bring.

But even as she had that thought, she pushed it away. She wasn't a foolish girl, and she knew better than to think such a thing. He'd affected her that night in a way she hadn't been able to forget. For her to think she could get away with having sex with him again without emotional consequences was a foolish notion.

Their dinner was finished and, with a full stomach and a slightly light head, Lexie felt the blissful awareness of sleepiness. If she could sleep the flight away she wouldn't have the damnable internal battle that wouldn't stop plaguing her. They were less than two hours into the flight and still had one stop and fifteen hours to go.

She accepted another vodka and tonic as she leaned back and closed her eyes. But her heart pounded as she thought about Lance being only two feet away from her. She could reach out, run her fingers over his hard thighs . . .

"Why don't you take advantage of the comfortable clothes in the back? You can even lie down in the bed for a while if you want," Lance said, his tone darkening as he said bed. Her heart thudded in response.

"I think I will," she told him with a squeak. She reached for her seat belt and her fingers were trembling so badly she wasn't able to get the dang latch undone. Without saying anything, Lance reached over and unclicked it, the back of his fingers rubbing against her thighs.

On trembling legs, Lexie stood up, praying there wouldn't be turbulence to knock her back down, and she turned to walk away. She had no idea where she was heading. But she felt Lance's hot breath on the back of her neck as she made her way down a long hallway with several doors. She wanted to ask how large the jet was, but she didn't.

A door was in the middle of the wall at the end of the hallway, and he reached around her, his body brushing her back as he hit the handle and pushed it open. She didn't move, relishing the feel of his body rubbing against hers for only a few fleeting seconds.

"The closet to the left of the bed has some items hanging. The drawers have clothing in them, too. The bathroom has toiletries, and you're free to take a shower if you want," he said, his hot breath brushing her ear, causing a shudder to run through her. She had no doubt he'd felt it.

Lance stood in the doorway for several seconds as she moved forward, her gaze straying to the large bed in the center of the room. If she had forgotten they were on a plane, she'd have thought this was a hotel room. It was larger than her apartment bedroom. The carpet was lush, the cabinets beautiful, and there were so many storage areas; she wished she had something similar.

The click of the door closing was a relief. She turned to make sure he was gone and then backed up and plopped down on the bed before her knees gave out and she ended up on the floor where she wasn't so sure she'd be able to get back up again.

Lexie didn't care how long she sat there. She didn't move until her breathing and heart rate were under control. The flight had barely begun and she was already a mess. It was an omen of a very long trip. With reluctance she stood, hating that her legs were still shaky.

Looking in the closet, she was shocked at how many clothes were available. She glanced at the tags and saw they were all her size. He'd been exactly right. She'd be able to change into a pair of yoga pants and comfortable top for the flight, then change into a new outfit of jeans and a sweater when they arrived.

When she opened a drawer and found delicate lace panties and bras she was horrified to see the sheerness and the coveted lingerie brand name. Those sizes were exactly right as well, which brought an image of his hands cupping her full breasts rushing through her mind.

She decided a shower was exactly what she needed. There was no way she was lying down in a bed that smelled like Lance, though. Her body could only be put through so much turmoil before she completely lost it.

Lexie took a hot shower in the surprisingly large bathroom and then took her time putting on lotion before she changed into the casual clothes. When she'd procrastinated long enough, she made her way back to the front of the plane where Lance was sitting comfortably, typing on a computer. The tray tables had been removed, leaving just the side table, complete with a refreshed drink. She also noticed how close their chairs were to each other. Should she move? No. That would tell him exactly how much his presence was affecting her.

She sat stiffly for a bit before she felt his gaze on her. Turning, the intensity in his eyes stunned her. His computer was forgotten as he lifted a hand and brushed a tendril of her damp hair away from her face. Lexie found herself wanting to run her tongue out and taste his fingertip that rubbed along her cheek before disappearing.

"I love that smell on you," he murmured. Her favorite lotion had been in the bathroom.

"How did you get everything exactly right?" she asked. She wasn't going to say the bras and panties fit perfectly. He grinned at her.

"I might have called your sister," he admitted.

Lexie decided right then and there, even though she loved Savvy, she would certainly have to kill her. Savvy had known she'd be going away with Lance and she hadn't warned her. What a traitor. They'd been in the bar for hours, and Savvy had been moaning and groaning about her leaving when she'd been aware of not only her departure, but of the fact that Lance was going as well.

"I'm going to have to talk to Savs," Lexie said with a clear threat in her tone.

Lance laughed. "Don't be too hard on her. She wanted this to be an amazing trip for you," he said, defending the traitor.

"She was complaining that I was going," she said.

"If she wouldn't have done so, then you might have grown suspicious," he pointed out.

"Suspicious of what?" she asked.

"That this might be a setup," he told her with a wink.

"*Is* this a setup?" she boldly asked.

"Maybe," he said, not even trying to hide his enthusiasm at it being just that.

"Yeah, my sister and I are definitely having a talk," she said.

Lance laughed again before he stood and leaned over her. Lexie decided she would allow a single kiss. That wouldn't hurt, she told herself. But he smiled again as if he could read her thoughts then reached over the side of her seat as he scooted back.

Her chair reclined and a footstool came out. Lance backed away and reached into a cupboard, pulling out a thick down blanket. The disappointment filtering through her was a shock. She didn't seem to know what it was she wanted.

"The blanket is warm," she said with appreciation as she pulled it around her.

"It was sitting in a heated cupboard," he told her.

Oh, this was most certainly the way to fly.

"You've spoiled me for ever flying in a regular plane again," she said, but there was zero heat in her words. Between the food, alcohol, and warmth of her seat, she was already giving in to exhaustion.

"That's the plan," she thought she heard him say, but she was already drifting off. Her last thought was that it was too bad he hadn't tried for that kiss.

CHAPTER FOUR

T HE SUN WAS slowly brightening the jet as fresh morning rays crept in through the window slats. Lance was leaning back in his chair while Lexie mumbled in her sleep, her head cradled against his chest as she shifted, her body seeking his in sleep. She'd been that way for the past couple hours, and Lance hadn't wanted to stir an inch for fear she'd wake and realize what she was doing.

She began growing more restless, and he knew she wouldn't sleep much longer, but they'd soon begin their descent into Manila, and he knew she'd want some time to change and get ready.

Unable to resist, he ran his hand across her high cheekbone and brushed her hair away from her face. She looked so peaceful in sleep. He hadn't been allowed the opportunity to enjoy the feel of her in his arms the one night they'd spent together. He'd woken to find her gone.

He'd often wondered if he'd been the first to wake, would things have worked out differently? Would they have made love again and then had a leisurely breakfast in bed before taking a walk together on the beach?

Lance wasn't normally one to think about what might have been, but when it came to Lexie he often wondered. He enjoyed her body, but he was also enthralled by her wit and charm. She was strong and stubborn and so damn beautiful. He couldn't find a single flaw in her. Lance didn't think it possible to find something that would make her less desirable in his eyes.

That was something new for him as well. He was normally better at finding problems with a potential partner than positive attributes. He'd been picky most of his life, but that was why he'd been able to accept his father's challenge so much easier than his siblings had been able to do. He had always liked a challenge. When he'd gotten over his initial anger, he'd gone with it fully and had surpassed his father's expectations, and his own.

Lance wanted this quiet piece of time with Lexie to last forever, but he knew the moment she was awake she would pull away from him and close up. For a few seconds she snuggled tighter against him, and he felt her body stir as she inhaled a deep breath. Then her body stiffened, and he ached as she pulled away.

Putting his chair into a seated position, he watched as her eyes fluttered and opened and then he felt that sense of peace again as they gazed at one another. A physical pang rushed through him at the need to reach for her, pull her into his lap, and hold her close. And he might have been able to get away with it for a few minutes, but he also knew it wouldn't last too long before she began easing away.

It really was too bad, but he reminded himself they were only at the beginning of their journey. They had a long way to go before they were back in the States where it would be easier for her to run from him.

"We're landing in about an hour. You can change and have breakfast with me," he suggested. He hadn't used his voice all night and there was a low growl to it. He felt a bit of pride at the desire flashing in her eyes.

Reaching up, he scratched his chin where stubble was poking through. He didn't shave every day when he came to work at one of his non-profits. It was nice to put on a worn pair of jeans, feel dirt on his hands, and let himself go a little.

"Thanks," she mumbled. Then she jumped up and practically ran away. Lance didn't mind the view of her exiting — not one bit, especially in yoga pants that hugged her curvy ass to perfection. Damn, he wanted to squeeze those fit cheeks of hers while she sat on him and they went for a ride together.

Lance cleaned up in another bathroom and by the time he finished, Lexie was out of the master bedroom. He went in and changed, then returned to sit with her where she was quieter than normal as they shared breakfast.

Lexie wouldn't look at him as the plane began descending, and he wondered if he'd overestimated his appeal with the woman. Was she freaked because of how she'd awoken, or was she truly horrified at spending so much time with him? He would find out sooner rather than later — because the two of them would be sharing a residence once they arrived. He'd rather they shared a room, but he wasn't going to push her that far — at least not yet.

Their landing was smooth, and Lance led her from the plane to a waiting car. He took the keys as his staff loaded their bags, including the items he'd bought for her — especially those delicate panties he wanted her to put on so he could then turn around and rip them off.

"Are you ready to see your home for the next thirty days?" Lance asked when they were alone in the small SUV.

"Yes, of course. I can't wait to dive into things," she said.

He hoped she still felt the same way when they arrived. The drive from the airport took about an hour, and though Lance had been to the place many times in the past few years, he still couldn't get over the beauty of the country. It was Lexie's first trip there, and her eyes were glued to her window as she tried to take it all in.

When they pulled up to the modest house on the outskirts of the small village his company had put so much time and money into, Lexie smiled in delight. She turned to look at him, for once without her guard up.

"Is this the place?" she asked.

Lance looked at the house, trying to see it through her eyes. It was so much smaller than his house back home, but it was quaint: a two-bedroom place, only about a thousand square feet with a small attached garage. He had crew members year-round in the area, and they often used the residence. She looked at it as though it were a mansion.

"I thought I'd be in a tent," she said with a chuckle. "I was prepared for that, and didn't mind at all. I *am* a bit of a baby when it comes to plumbing though," she admitted.

"Let me give you the grand tour," he suggested.

"Where are you staying?" she asked him as they stepped from the vehicle and walked up the short path to the front door. He decided to ignore her question for at least a few minutes. He would let her freak out about their living situation soon enough.

He opened the door, and she forgot the question as she smiled at each little thing in the place. It was modestly furnished with no television, but he'd installed satellite Internet as he couldn't go without it for more than a day at most. Sometimes he wished he could, but he feared the world really would fall apart without him. Maybe that was a little bit of an ego stroke, but he liked to think that way.

"You'll be sleeping here," he said as he opened the door to a small bedroom with a queen-size bed taking up most of the room. She smiled as if she'd won a lottery as she practically glided inside the room and sat on the bed, the mattress giving her a bit of a bounce. He hadn't skimped on cheap sleeping arrangements. Lance had once been told the average person spent a third of their life in bed. To him, that made it worth the investment in high-quality bedding.

"This is perfect, Lance, just perfect. I promised my sister I would only be gone a month, but this place is so much better than my apartment. I might never want to go back," she said with a laugh. "I haven't seen a real wood stove in what feels like a million years. I can't wait to get a fire started."

"It's a bit warm for fires," he pointed out. Though back home it was cold and dreary, here it was in the seventies, and expected to get warmer before they left.

"It's never too warm for a fire," she countered.

He grinned at her, desperately wanting to walk over, push her down, and climb on top of her. He wasn't sure he'd be able to hold himself back — especially after being with her night after night.

"You really don't have to stick around. You can just tell me where I'm supposed to be at what time, or leave me a schedule like the board told me I would get, and then you can get settled," she said. "We both have to unpack."

"I don't have far to go," he told her, his voice a bit tight. He wished she'd either get off the damn bed she looked ready to make love to, or strip and let him in with her. His voice must have alerted her because her grin fell, and she gave him a wary glance.

"Where exactly is not far?" she asked.

He leaned in the doorjamb as he smiled at her.

"About two feet," he said, watching for her reaction. He had to give her credit because he might not have noticed how affected she was if he couldn't read her eyes so damn well.

"Like right next door?" she asked, with what sounded like hopefulness in her tone.

"Next door to your room, yes," he answered.

She opened her mouth like she wanted to say something, and then she shut it again. This happened several times before words actually came out.

"You're staying in the *same* house?" she squeaked.

"Yep," he told her. "I better unpack."

He didn't give her time to respond to that little piece of information. He just turned and walked the couple of feet to his own bedroom, shut the door, and leaned on it. He was putting himself through hell for this woman. Yes, he'd stayed in this place before but never for more than a couple days, and certainly not with a beautiful woman who was completely unattainable — or so it seemed.

The bedrooms didn't even have their own bathrooms. He hadn't wanted to make something lavish in the impoverished area, so he'd kept it simple. It was still nicer than a lot of the places large families lived in. He'd gone as small as possible without hitting his elbows and knees on the walls. The bathroom did have a large shower. He couldn't give up that luxury, but at least there was no tub. There weren't a lot of extras. Lance considered the place to be a camping adventure, making him realize he was a lot more spoiled than he had thought.

Lexie was enthralled with the place, and he wanted to get out of it as quickly as possible. There was a nice hotel he stayed in about an hour away. But when he came into the village they were rebuilding, he always felt guilty about living a life of luxury while the children he'd gotten to know were so grateful for something as simple as fresh bread.

Still, the house could be five thousand square feet and feel like a tin box as long as he was alone with Lexie but unable to touch her. He might have put himself into a situation he would forever regret.

Lance had often been told a person should never regret a decision they'd made, that everything had a reason behind it, and even failures were there to make you a stronger person. He might be repeating that sentiment to himself a lot over the next few weeks. He certainly would as he took a shower every day, knowing Lexie had been in the same place — naked, soapy, and wet.

With a groan, Lance threw himself down on the bed and closed his eyes, his body throbbing and fully aware that relief was only one door away. He hoped for both their sakes she didn't resist him too long.

If so, he might have to kidnap the woman and sex her into submission.

CHAPTER FIVE

ONE NIGHT DOWN, twenty-nine to go, Lexie assured herself as she exited the shower and wrapped a towel around her freshly washed body. She'd been frustrated to find out she'd be sharing the same small house with Lance and felt she'd been set up. Then she felt guilty about having those thoughts.

They were in an area that had been ravaged by storms. She couldn't expect each of them to stay in big houses while islanders were sleeping in tents. How selfish could she actually be? She'd just have to suck it up. She'd had many roommates during college. It made living so much more affordable.

Of course she hadn't had an incredibly sexy roommate she wanted to be tied to a bed by before, but she would just have to get over those thoughts. Lexie stood with her ear pressed against the door for several moments as she waited to see if she could hear Lance. She hadn't even thought about bringing her clothes into the bathroom; at home she always showered, then went to her room to dress. She didn't have to worry about walking around with only a towel on. She often wore it into the kitchen while she put on a fresh pot of coffee.

But if she wanted to keep things professional between her and Lance, she wouldn't be able to do things like that. She didn't want the man to think she was a tease, or something even worse. On the other hand, he *had* seen her fully naked, so a towel was a lot of covering, considering.

She heard no sounds, so she creaked the door open and peeked out. He was nowhere to be found. Her heart pounding, she opened the door and made a mad dash to her bedroom, her heart not slowing until she was on the other side of the closed door, her towel still in place.

What a way to start off the day. She wasn't going to last a month like this. She was sure of it. But she couldn't imagine the very spoiled Lance Storm surviving in what she assumed he'd think was a lesser place than he was used to.

The house was ideal to her, more than she could have ever expected; her own apartment was so small she could practically reach her arms out and touch each wall. Maybe that was a slight exaggeration, but Lexie was used to living meagerly, and she didn't mind it one bit. She had a strong work ethic, and paid her own way, and that said something about a person, she'd decided long ago. Maybe she had commitment issues, but everyone had to have at least a few skeletons in their secret closet.

Getting dressed, Lexie made her way to the kitchen, thrilled when she found a fresh pot of coffee. She didn't want to admit her disappointment in finding the kitchen empty. The last thing she needed was to grow attached to seeing Lance. They were doing a job together and that was all. She didn't want, nor need, to see his face, especially first thing in the morning.

Sitting down with a fresh cup of coffee and a bagel with cream cheese, she was startled when Lance joined her, turning a chair around and straddling it like she wouldn't mind straddling him. Shaking her head, she pushed that thought right back into the gutter where it belonged.

"Good morning. Are you looking forward to the day?" he asked as he sipped his coffee.

"Yes. I didn't find the schedule though, so I have no idea what we're doing," she pointed out. She'd lost her appetite but forced herself to eat anyway. She wasn't sure when she'd get a chance for more fuel, and she planned on working hard so she'd definitely need the energy the food would provide.

"I've got the schedule right here," he said with a smile as he pointed to his head.

"I would prefer it on paper," she said, not amused.

"What fun would that be? Waste not, want not," he told her.

"I'm here to do a job, Lance, *not* play games with you," she huffed.

"Why can't we do both?" he asked with dripping innocence.

"Can you at least tell me *when* we're going?" she said, her own voice sugary sweet. Two could play that game, she decided.

"As soon as you finish your meal," he told her.

Though the bagel now tasted like sawdust, Lexie washed it down with coffee. She normally wouldn't mind another cup while she sat back and looked through her phone, but she feared she'd go a little insane if she stayed in the house with Lance for too long.

"Ready," she told him after she got up and rinsed her cup. "Are these clothes okay?"

Lance took the opportunity to look at her from head to toe and she regretted her choice of words as his intense stare caused her to heat up in all the wrong places — okay, the right places, wrong man, she corrected.

"You look perfect," he said in a low purr.

"This isn't a fashion statement. I need to know what I'm doing so I can be prepared," she told him.

"Today, we're going to the village to meet the kids," he said. "Comfort is what you want to dress for. You're going to be on your feet a lot, and we'll be doing many different tasks."

Lexie really wished the man wouldn't smile so much. It was so much harder to resist their chemistry when he looked at her like she was his next meal. And the open smile that said to the world he was a happy-go-lucky kind of guy was nearly her undoing.

"Good because that's the sort of clothes I brought," she said. "I looked up the temps and knew it would be warmer here."

"I wouldn't mind getting you a bikini or two if you want a day off at the beach," he said with a waggle of his brows.

If they were at the beach together, that would mean he'd be wearing shorts — and nothing else. Damn, she wouldn't mind that. Nope. Shaking her head she gave him what she hoped was a friendly smile.

"I'm good. Let's go," she said as she walked to the front door.

Lance led her from the house and instead of getting in the vehicle he grabbed her hand and led her down a dirt road. She tried tugging free of him for a few seconds, but gave up when it was obvious he wasn't unhanding her.

They walked along silently for several minutes before she allowed her body to relax. She didn't want to think about how right it felt to have her fingers safely held in his strong grip. She could get way too comfortable with the situation, and that wasn't a good thing at all.

"When did you decide you wanted to be a part of the recovery efforts?" Lance asked her.

She took a moment to think about it. She knew exactly when she'd decided, but she didn't know if she wanted to share her tortured past with him. That would open doors she knew were best left closed.

"I don't know," she finally said. "I guess I have just seen a lot of suffering in the world and since I'm single and available, I thought I could help. I don't have any particular knowledge or skills, but I do love helping others, and I have a passion to do what's right, so that makes up for it — or at least I tell myself that," she said with a laugh.

Lance stopped and turned her so she was forced to look in his eyes. She shifted uncomfortably as he looked at her like he could see all the way into her soul.

"The wealthiest and most skilled people in the world start off with nothing but passion and drive. Don't underestimate yourself," he told her.

This conversation had quickly taken a path she wasn't at all prepared to walk down. She finally broke the connection of their eyes and forced a laugh.

"Maybe you should be a motivational speaker. That was very inspiring," she said.

He took her chin in his fingers and gazed at her a moment longer. He didn't say a word, but she knew she hadn't fooled him with her uncomfortable words. He shook his head, but then that natural light returned to his eyes.

"We'll revisit this," he promised. He took her hand again, and the two of them continued walking.

Turning a corner, she heard voices before she saw a crowd. Seeing all the people, her heart swelled with joy and pride. Lexie had visited many places in the States, and she'd always enjoyed being where disaster had struck, seeing the hope and gratefulness on people's faces. Even though they'd been through terrible circumstances, they continued to look at the positive; they were alive and with their families. She wasn't sure she could hold on to the same enthusiasm if she were in their place. She hoped she could.

But the people looked happy and cheerful, though there didn't seem to be much to earn that enthusiasm. What did Lexie really know about what brought people true joy? Each person was different. That's what made the world so great.

"Lance," a young boy called out, and several children who had formed a makeshift baseball field in the middle of the village turned, their faces lighting up as she and Lance approached.

"Hello, Arnel, how are you doing, buddy?" Lance asked as he let go of her hand and knelt just in time for the young boy to fling himself into Lance's arms.

"I'm good," Arnel replied, squeezing Lance tightly. Before Lance could say anything else, the rest of the kids reached them and began climbing all over Lance, until they finally toppled him to the ground.

The sound of Lance's laughter came through loud and clear, and Lexie felt a thump in her heart at how beautiful the moment was. Before she realized what she was doing, her phone was in her hand and she was snapping pictures of the mob. Lance looked up with sparkling eyes and a wide grin as her camera clicked, and that distance Lexie was trying to put between the two of them shortened just a little more.

The man had obviously spent quite a bit of time in this small village, and it was more than obvious that the kids knew and loved him. How could she keep her distance from a man who was loved by so many who had so little? It wasn't going to be an easy task.

"We're playing baseball like you taught us," another of the boys said. "Will you join us?"

"Of course, Rey," Lance replied. "Do you mind if my friend, Lexie, joins us?"

The group of young boys turned their attention toward Lexie, and she felt as if she were being judged — and came up lacking. It wasn't her most comfortable moment, but she smiled reassuringly at the kids.

"I would love to join you," she said, her voice hopeful. She felt like she was back in the third grade, hoping to not be chosen last for the team during P.E.

"I *guess* she can play. Does she know how to hit?" Arnel asked with doubt.

"I don't know. I guess we'll find out," Lance told the kids. They finally allowed him to stand up.

"I played softball in college. I can hit," Lexie assured the kids.

A couple of the children whispered to each other, giving her an assessing look.

"I'll take her on my team," another boy said quietly as he kicked the dirt with what looked like brand new sneakers. Lexie wondered how much Lance did for these kids, how much he provided.

"Thanks," Lexie said as she kneeled down. "I'm Lexie. What's your name?"

The boy, who couldn't have been more than eight years old, looked up and gave her a tentative smile. "I'm Edwin," he said.

"That's a great name. I think we're going to beat Lance and his team," she told the boy with enthusiasm. That made him smile.

The teams formed quickly and Lexie found herself pitching. She went nice and easy and her team groaned when the other team got big hits and made their way around the bases. She laughed with joy as they slid into home plate and did victory dances.

Then Lance was standing at the plate and she got into a pitcher formation.

"Don't take it easy on me, Lex," Lance told her.

"Wouldn't dream of it," she replied with a wicked gleam. She'd been holding her best stuff back.

The first ball flew by him at a speed that almost knocked her catcher over. She was about to apologize when the boy looked at her with brand new admiration in his eyes.

"Wow," he said. "Do that again."

Lexie met Lance's surprised gaze, and she winked at him. That made his lips twitch as he got more comfortable at home plate. Then a challenge entered his expression.

"I didn't know we were trying out for the all-stars," Lance said. He shifted his feet and Lexie grew nervous. This man looked good at anything he did, but standing there holding a bat with two days' worth of stubble on his face was about the sexiest thing she'd seen in a while — hell, that she'd ever seen, if she were going to be honest with herself.

The next ball came out of her hand just as fast as the first one, but this time he was ready for it. He swung and smashed the small ball. It went over her head and down the road with kids chasing after it.

The kids on base ran as if their lives depended on it, and Lance took off in a slow jog, rounding the bases as the kids called out to each other. The catcher took off down the third base line and Lance was rounding third for home, so Lexie ran up to protect it as the ball was lobbed toward home.

She caught it just as Lance reached her, and she grinned at him as he went down into a slide. Kneeling, she touched his foot just before it connected with the base and then her feet. She was going down.

"You're out," she called as she toppled over on top of him. Lance was laughing as his arms caged around her, softening the impact as she landed on his solid body.

"The ump calls the outs," he told her, his arms caging her in.

Lexie forgot she was in the middle of a game with a bunch of screaming kids around them. She forgot she was in a foreign country, forgot she was to stay away from this man. She forgot everything, even how to breathe, as his laughter died away and awareness shot through his vibrant gaze.

"Good job, Ace," Lance said before his hand drifted up to the back of her head. Lexie was so close to caving in and leaning down, accepting the offer in his eyes. Her head began to descend when a loud voice interrupted them.

"You're out," the ump yelled, waking Lexie up to the reality of their situation.

She turned, her body still fully pressed against Lance, the evidence of his hunger pushing up between her thighs.

"Bad timing," Lance muttered, disappointment lacing through his words.

"I'd say that's perfect timing," Lexie disagreed as she pushed against him.

With a reluctant sigh and one more scorching look, Lance released her. Lexie scrambled to her feet on shaking knees, grateful that was the last out. She needed to go and sit on the dirt road for a bit before she fell over.

Day two was even more of a mess than day one. This trip was growing more and more impossible by the minute.

CHAPTER SIX

L ANCE TOOK A nice long shower, washing away the day's dirt. Fifteen minutes in, he was still hard and throbbing, and he thought about doing something about it, but the idea of relieving himself while Lexie was only a room away was far too unappealing, so he switched the shower to cold and pointed it directly at the part of his body that was so damn neglected.

He promised himself to do something about that neglect very soon. Of course he had to get Lexie on board to make it happen. He saw the desire in her eyes, and he didn't think it would be too big a problem if she'd just quit fighting herself. She was scared. He got that. He'd been afraid of anything resembling commitment for a very long time. It was how the world worked.

Getting himself in a somewhat manageable state, he stepped from the shower, goose bumps covering his skin. Drying off quickly, he put on clothes, then opened the door to the bathroom and was assaulted with delicious smells that led him straight to the kitchen.

He stopped and listened to dance music playing. Lexie was at the stove stirring something as her hips swayed to a song. She did a shuffle on her feet and his eyes were glued to her perfect ass as it swiveled when she did a little roll of her hips.

And just like that, he was throbbing again. Shifting on his feet, he watched her for several minutes as his pants grew increasingly uncomfortable. She began to sing along with the song when the chorus started, and he leaned against the wall and grinned. Her dance moves were far more impressive than her voice, but damn if he didn't find her the sexiest woman he'd ever witnessed.

Slowly, he approached her, too mesmerized to stay away any longer. He wanted this woman with a passion that bordered on insanity. They were together in this small house, and he could think of a million ways to make the stay more pleasant for both of them.

"Need any help?" he whispered as he leaned down and inhaled her sweet scent. He swore he could taste peaches and he wanted to swipe his tongue along the soft skin of her neck, maybe even take a bite. He wasn't pressed against her, but one small step forward and she would be in his arms. Damn, he wanted to take that step.

"I've got it," she choked out. She was just as affected as he was. He really wanted to turn her around, press her against the counter, and take her right there. He'd buy her new clothes after he ripped the ones she was wearing off her luscious body.

"Are you sure? I'm really good at . . . helping," he said, his lips millimeters from her skin. Just one taste he thought as he leaned a bit closer and pressed his nose to her neck. Yes, definitely peaches — and he only wanted a small taste.

"You can put the salad together," she said as a shudder went through her body that made him nearly come undone. He wanted to push into her, make her surrender to him, but with superhuman effort he backed away and went to the fridge, pulling out vegetables.

Over the next fifteen minutes, he brushed against her every chance he could, reaching for spices and utensils, and did a terrible job of getting a salad put together. Lexie's breathing deepened as she tried to stay unaffected by it all, but he could practically read her body better than he could his own, and he knew she was hungry for a lot more than the food she was preparing.

She was making a stew that smelled almost as good as she did. But Lance had only one appetite at the moment that needed satisfied. He had so many fantasies of taking her at every place in the small house that he was beginning to lose his grip on reality. He also decided that might not be such a bad thing. Living in a fantasy world could be a lot more fun than the painful reality he found himself in. Could he add in some role-play and maybe a mask too? Nah. All he needed was Lexie's naked body, and he would most certainly be a happy man.

"It's ready," Lexie said, pulling him back to reality. This was going to be a painful dinner.

He helped her set the table then sat beside her as the two of them shared a delicious meal he barely tasted.

"Did you enjoy yourself today?" he asked.

"It wasn't what I was expecting," she said with a smile, finally meeting his gaze.

"What do you mean?"

"I thought we'd be doing work," she said with a chuckle.

"Part of what we do is to be there for the kids. They start to work young here, and to have a day of play is a welcome relief," he told her.

"I guess I have always thought of you as all work and no play," she admitted. That stung a little bit. There had been a time when Lance had been all or nothing, whether it was working or playing. Now he liked to think he'd learned a lot about balance in his life.

"There's always time for both," he told her. He was thinking of all sorts of ways he could play with her right now.

"I agree. Sometimes I forget that it doesn't have to be one or the other," she said with a sigh.

Before long, their plates were empty. Maybe he'd been hungrier than he'd thought.

"Did you get enough?" she asked. "I wasn't sure if we were cooking separately or what, and I don't normally cook for another person. If I had that schedule I'd know more," she said as she stood up and began taking plates to the kitchen.

"We can take turns cooking. It doesn't make sense for each of us to make our own food," he told her as he followed her into the kitchen.

"Okay," she said with what sounded like relief.

"This doesn't have to be complicated," he said, grabbing her hand before she turned on the faucet. He wanted her to look into his eyes, to show her he was talking about more than just a meal schedule.

She met his gaze, and he saw acceptance for a blink of an eye before she placed shutters over her expression and reached for the faucet again. He wanted to scream in agony.

"Of course not, but I do better when I know what I'm facing," she said. He wondered if there was a double meaning behind that sentence.

"I can accept that," he said. Should he just tell her how much he wanted her? Stop talking in riddles? Lance was unsure, and he didn't like feeling that way — not one bit.

"I can do these," Lexie told him, her voice nervous.

"You cooked the meal, we can do the dishes together."

Their hands met in the sink as they cleaned up their small mess, and Lance's body grew harder and harder the longer he stood next to her. It was both heaven and hell having her so close he could smell her, practically taste her.

Lexie was drying the last dish when they both moved at the same time, his body fully brushing against hers. She looked up, their eyes connected, and he felt his heart pounding so hard, it felt as if it were trying to rip itself from his chest.

"Screw it," he muttered before taking the dish from her and tossing it somewhere behind her on the counter.

Her breathing stopped as he backed her into the cupboards, his hands lifting and sifting through her soft hair. "I want you so much," he breathed against her lips. Her breath rushed out against his mouth.

He didn't give her a chance to protest this time but reached for her hips and squeezed before lifting her to the counter. A small whimper escaped her open mouth before their lips connected.

Pure bliss filtered through him as he traced her mouth, easily diving inside to consume her the way he'd wanted to for days — hell, for over a year if he was telling the truth.

His fingers fisted in her hair as she moaned into his mouth. He grew hungrier as he pulled her to the edge of the counter, pressing his body against hers, his solidness easily pushing against her heat. He pulsed against her, wishing they didn't have clothing in the way.

He needed to be buried inside her while his mouth captured hers. He wanted all clothing gone so he could relieve the ache they were both feeling so desperately. He feared one touch of her hand against his throbbing erection would have him coming like a teen in the back of his dad's old Ford pickup.

Lance wanted to shout with joy when her hands climbed up his arms and locked behind his neck as she pushed her breasts against him. He wanted to taste and touch every inch of her like he'd done the night of the wedding, wanted to consume her so fully she wouldn't have time to think of resisting.

His hand left her hair and traveled down her trembling body until he found the hem of her shirt. Slipping his hand inside, he delighted in the feel of her satin skin as he trailed his fingers up her side, loving the feel of her trembling beneath his touch. His fingers whispered over the side of her lacy bra, and his hunger grew fiercer.

She groaned against his mouth as he scooted back enough to slip his hand over the cup of her breast and squeeze the sensitive flesh. Her nipple poked against her bra and he rubbed his palm against her, making her squirm on the counter in front of him.

Slipping his fingers beneath the bra, he nearly came in his pants, feeling her hot flesh in his hand. She cried out in his mouth when he squeezed her nipple, and then she began shaking in his arms.

"Lance . . ." she groaned, her mouth wrenching from his. He trailed his lips down her neck, sucking the skin before he scooted back enough to tug her shirt over her head. He continued trailing his lips down her chest until he reached her beautiful breasts. He just needed a little taste, he assured himself.

There was a clasp on the front of her bra, and he was able to undo it with a flick of his fingers. Her breasts spilled into his palms, and he pulsed in his pants. He didn't stop the journey of his mouth until he was latched onto her nipple. When he sucked it into his hot mouth, she cried out again, and he felt her shaking as he bit down.

She tensed and then let out another cry as he sucked one nipple and squeezed the other. Then she went limp in his arms. Shocked, he kissed his way back up her body and traced her lips with his tongue. Her eyes were dilated as she met his gaze. She'd come from little more than his kiss and the feel of his mouth on her nipples. He was in awe of this beautiful, sexual creature.

He wanted to give her one orgasm after another. He had forgotten about his own need for a moment. She leaned against him as if their connection was too great; she couldn't look at him any longer. For just this moment in time he wanted to do nothing more than hold her.

But as she squirmed in his arms, his own need came raging to the surface. He pulled back, afraid she was going to leave him. He wasn't sure he could survive that. When she looked at him again, she gave him an assessing gaze, and then she pushed against his chest.

Lance wanted to find a weapon and end his own life right then and there. He wasn't sure he would survive her rejection at this point.

"Your turn," she whispered. Lance didn't understand what she was saying until she jumped down from the counter and knelt at his feet. He wanted to stop her. This wasn't a contest. She didn't owe him an orgasm because he'd given her one.

But then her fingers were on the waistband of his sweats, and she was tugging them down. He tried to open his mouth to tell her she didn't need to do this, but then the cool air hit his throbbing skin seconds before her hot breath rushed over him, and he lost the ability to speak.

When her mouth closed over his pulsing flesh, a gurgle of sound escaped him before his fingers were tugging on her hair.

She pulled him deep into her mouth, wetting him, making him drip his pleasure on her tongue, lubricating the path.

She sucked him deep while squeezing him with her hand. He groaned in ecstasy as she brought him closer to the relief he needed so desperately. When she pulled him from her mouth and ran her tongue along his length he knew it was almost over. He wanted to be buried inside her, but he couldn't pull away from her incredible mouth.

She sucked on him again, and he pulled her hair hard as an explosion ripped through him. His release coated her tongue as he shook beneath her touch. He pulsed over and over again, a guttural sound emerging from him as she held him tight and continued to suck him.

When the orgasm was over, he opened his eyes and looked down. She was gazing up at him with satisfaction. Her tongue came out and licked her swollen lips, and some of his pleasure dripped from the corner of her mouth, making him ready for a second orgasm.

He wanted this woman with unlimited passion. He knew it would never be enough. It didn't matter how many times he took her, it would never be enough. But he sure as hell would try to have her as much as possible.

He reached down and lifted her to her feet, needing to take her lips. A salty flavor resided there, but he didn't care. He was falling for her in so many ways he would never be able to end the connection.

She pulled back and smiled at him before lifting her hand and brushing sweat from his brow. Then she pushed away, and he felt instant coldness where she'd been pressed against him.

"I'm not going to say I didn't want that because I did," she said. But he was watching the shutters come over her eyes. He didn't like that at all. He wanted to give her so much pleasure she wouldn't have time for regrets.

"But . . ." he said, knowing it was coming.

"But it won't continue," she told him. The final board was nailed into place on the coffin burying him in the ground.

He knew he could fight her, knew he could get her into his bed. But he didn't want it to be a fight. He wanted her to come willingly.

"It will," he said as he reached up and cupped her face. "But I'm a patient man."

Lexie looked at him with shock. Good. He wanted to surprise her. If she thought she knew him, she would learn there was much more to him than what met the eye. He was in this for the long haul. He decided that right then. He wasn't sure he'd ever let this woman go.

He didn't stop her when she turned and walked away from him. He had plenty of time to woo her. That thought made him smile. He'd never had to woo a woman before. What an old-fashioned term. He decided he liked it a lot. He'd get her into his bed, and he hoped to hell he got into her heart.

CHAPTER SEVEN

SWEAT BEADED OFF Lexie's brow as she swung a hammer and nearly hit her thumb. Snatching her hand back, she cursed and looked around to make sure a kid was nowhere in sight. Thankfully none were.

Two weeks! She'd been in this village in the Philippines for two long weeks, and after that second night when things had gotten hot and heavy in the small house she shared with Lance, the steam had gone depressingly down.

It was what she wanted, she convinced herself. She didn't need to have a steamy affair with the man. Her brain was on the right track, but her body wasn't listening. She lay in bed night after night wondering if he was awake, if he was touching himself the way she wanted to touch him. She wondered if she was going to survive living side by side with the man.

He seemed to take every opportunity to touch her, tease her, smile, and flirt with her, without taking it to the next level. The morning after their steamy counter make-out session he'd told her he would respect what she wanted; he wouldn't push her to do more than she was willing to do. He'd also told her all she had to do was say the word and the two of them could be sharing a bed.

She hated her damn stubbornness, hated that she was resisting what she wanted so badly. But Lexie feared that if she gave in to the hunger of wanting him, gave in to her body's desire, she would never be able to turn things around. She feared she would fall in love with the man, and then she'd be in an entirely different world of hurt.

She could last a couple more weeks in this country, watching him as he worked hard bringing things to families who were so appreciative. If he were a monster this would be easy. She would allow herself to let go and take comfort in his arms. But he was anything but a devil. He was kind and generous, and he was the type of man she hadn't thought truly existed. He was the kind of man a woman wanted to keep forever.

But Lexie didn't trust herself — didn't trust that what she was feeling was real. She was seeing one side of him. But her dad had also been able to lay on the charm, not that he'd bothered to do it very often and certainly not for as long a stretch as Lance was doing. But that fear was still there. Lance could change, and when that happened it might be too late for her to shift her own feelings toward him.

So instead of taking what she wanted — what he'd offered to give her — she suffered each and every day. It wasn't going too well for her, but he seemed fine, happy as could be, in fact.

Lexie's gaze searched the area they were working, and she found Lance without much effort. He was putting together a shed, his shirt off, his tanned skin gleaming in the sun. Back home it would be rainy, possibly even icy, but where they were the sun was shining and the temperatures were in the high seventies to low eighties, which wasn't helping with her situation at all.

Lexie was getting ready to turn away and get back to work when she saw a beautiful brunette approach Lance with a cup and a smile, her hips swaying in the short shorts she wore, her upper half barely covered by an indecent bikini top. Lexie glared at the woman, who was unaware of the heated gaze sent her way. Hell, the woman was only focused on Lance.

Without realizing she was moving, Lexie stepped closer, staying hidden behind the house as she spied on them. She couldn't hear what was being said, but she could see it all, and when Lance threw his head back and laughed, and the woman reached out and ran her fingernail down his naked chest, Lexie felt her claws come out.

She had no reason to feel jealous, no right to stake a claim, but that's exactly how she felt and what she wanted to do. Lexie hadn't seen this woman around the village before and didn't like that she was invading what Lexie considered *her* space.

Lance drank whatever the woman had brought — probably something with a roofie in it — and some of the drink dribbled down his chin. Lexie didn't have to worry about that, because the woman reached up and wiped the moisture away with her thumb before she pulled her hand back and licked the digit in a very inappropriate way.

Lexie didn't believe in calling names or shaming other women, but there were a few choice words she wanted to call the brunette, who wasn't trying to hide the fact that she wanted to jump Lance's bones. He was obviously enjoying the moment, and it solidified in Lexie's mind that she'd made the right decision in not getting involved with the man.

Whether he was sleeping with Lexie or not, he would constantly have women throw themselves at him, and she couldn't compete with that. She didn't want to pretend to be someone other than who she was to keep him faithful. She shouldn't have to be a different person to keep her man interested. Not that Lance was her man she reminded herself.

Unable to watch the scene anymore, she turned away. It had been a long day and she was done. There was no way she'd be able to watch him walk off with the woman — probably to go to her place, or to some private area on the beach not too far away.

The thought made Lexie's stomach heave, and she had to fight back the feeling of nausea. This was too much for her to take. Sadness filtered through her as she skirted the couple before beginning the walk back to the place she was sharing with Lance.

When she reached the door to their house another horrifying thought came to mind. What if he brought the woman home? He wouldn't do that, would he? There was no way he was so clueless that he would flaunt another woman in the place Lexie was staying.

Fear filled her at the thought. If he brought that woman home, Lexie's claws would surely come out as she attacked. The thought was so horrifying she felt her body trembling with rage.

What in the world was wrong with her? She had to pull herself together. Maybe it was because it was getting closer to Christmas, but it didn't feel like it with such warm weather surrounding her. She wasn't sure. Maybe she needed more releases like what he'd given her a couple weeks before. Whatever it was, she had to get herself under control or she was never going to survive this trip.

Unable to push thoughts of Lance from her mind, she climbed into the shower and did something she hadn't done in a long time — she allowed herself to let go and have a good cry. Not even that helped.

CHAPTER EIGHT

"**I** HAVE A SURPRISE for you," Lance said as he joined Lexie in the kitchen the next morning.

She knew she was acting like a bratty child, but she couldn't help it. The night before she had taken her time cooking a nice dinner — and then she'd waited. She'd tried telling herself she wasn't waiting, but that was exactly what she'd been doing. She'd nibbled on her food with zero appetite, and she'd thrown out the rest, deciding if he wasn't going to come back to their place at a decent hour then the man didn't need to eat.

When she knew it would be pathetic for her to be sitting there waiting for him to come home, she'd gone to her room and tried to get lost in a book. That hadn't worked either. She'd been awake when she'd heard him come in, walking around the house about ten that evening. She'd been listening for the sound of another set of footsteps, which she hadn't heard.

Now it was morning and she was tired, grumpy, and in no mood to deal with any of his riddles. She wanted to punch him, and Lexie wasn't normally a violent woman, but Lance Storm brought out the worst in her. Maybe that was another reason she would be foolish to get involved in any sort of relationship with him.

"I don't want anything from you," she told him, unable to keep her anger from showing. Her tone stopped him in his tracks, and he gave her an assessing look. Dammit, she didn't want him to know how jealous she was. She wanted him to go back into his box where he didn't matter to her. She feared that wasn't going to happen anytime soon.

"What's wrong?" he asked as he sat down across from her, his face looking concerned. That was just more proof the man could act.

"Nothing's wrong. I don't want anything from you, especially any surprises," she said, this time able to more convincingly control her voice.

He looked at her for several moments before he reached across the table for her hand. She jerked it back so fast her coffee sloshed over her cup, some spilling on her. She screeched as the hot liquid burned her skin.

Lance was quick on his feet, jumping up and forcing her to release her death grip on the mug before dragging her over to the sink where he held her hand under cold water. She was stiff as he pressed against her.

"Let me get some ice. Keep your hand under the water for a while longer," he demanded. There was no other word for it. *He* now seemed irritated as he moved to the freezer and pulled out ice, wrapping it in a towel before coming back to her.

He turned off the faucet and led her to the table. Her hand wasn't hurting, thanks to his quick thinking, but she didn't feel like thanking him. All she could see was his hands all over the brunette's body, and the more she thought about it the more rage she felt.

"You are going to have to tell me what has you so riled up. As intelligent as I am, I've never claimed to be a mind reader," Lance said as he moved his chair so he was facing her as she held the towel on her hand.

"Nothing has me riled. I can say I don't want something without it being a big deal," she grumbled. The more she spoke the more absurd she knew she sounded. But if she told him what her problem was, then he would realize she was jealous and irrational, and she would rather cut off one of her right toes than admit to that.

Lance gave her a quizzical look before leaning back. He was assessing her, which made her squirm in her seat. This situation grew worse by the minute. She wanted to get up and run away.

"Okay, well, I'll tell you the surprise anyway," he said. "If you want to sit there and pout like a child, there's nothing I can do about it."

"What?" she screeched, hating the whine in her voice. "I'm not the one behaving like a horny adolescent."

"What's that supposed to mean?" he snapped.

"It doesn't matter. I'm not your keeper," she muttered.

When a smile lit up his face, she saw red and again felt the need to scratch the man's eyes out. She apparently couldn't keep her mouth shut. That was her problem; she was too much of an open book.

"This doesn't have anything to do with me getting in late does it?" he asked. The knowing tone of his voice had her on edge.

"Of course not. I have no idea what time you got in," she said too quickly.

Lance laughed and Lexie seriously contemplated picking up the rest of her coffee and tossing it in his face. Of course then she'd have to doctor him since he'd probably be blind. Still might be worth it.

"I was out with some of the guys having a drink and talking about a project," he told her.

"I didn't ask where you were," she said, but the flood of relief that filtered through her had her more worried than before. She wanted to demand to know that he hadn't gone anywhere with the brunette, but she wasn't going to do that. Besides, he could be making it all up. Men were pigs. They could easily go from one woman's bed to another.

"I think you're jealous," he said with wonder.

"I'm not jealous. There's nothing to be upset about," she yelled as she sent him a death glare.

"This is interesting," he said as if talking to himself and not her. She was growing closer to tossing that coffee.

"There's nothing interesting because I'm not jealous. I don't care who you're with or where you're at. You can be out all night if you want," she told him.

He looked at her again as he leaned back in his chair, and she could see the wheels turning. Then his smile turned to mega-wattage status, and she felt her fingers twitching toward the coffee cup.

"I didn't even think about it, but you disappeared shortly after I was talking to Bella," he said.

Bella! Of course the woman had a name like that. It was a floozy name, Lexie decided. Except she'd always sort of liked the name before hearing it come from Lance's lips while talking about a scantily clad woman. But now she decided it was definitely a hussy name.

"I don't know what you're talking about. I finished what I was doing, and I was hot so I left. I didn't think I needed to check in with you on my comings and goings," she muttered.

"You know, Lexie, you're the only woman I see anymore," he said. The seriousness in his voice nearly floored her.

"I don't expect that," she said. She was feeling pettier by the moment, and it wasn't a feeling she was enjoying. "You shouldn't be thinking about me because we are just partners here."

"Bella is a flirt, but it's all harmless. She wasn't around long," he told her. She wanted to jump up and hug the man, but then she would be admitting to him that she *had* been jealous and she hadn't slept because of it. It sounded as if he was telling her the truth. Lexie wasn't sure of anything in her current hormonal state.

"You don't need to explain things to me, Lance," she said, desperately wanting to get off the subject. "What is the surprise?"

"I thought you didn't want anything," he said with that standard grin.

"I don't. But I figure you won't shut up about it until you tell me, so I'm simply trying to shorten this conversation," she lied.

The look he gave her told her she wasn't fooling him at all. She hoped he kept that to himself. She wasn't sure how much more she could take before she had a complete breakdown and started blathering everything right then and there.

"Okay, I'll let you off the hook," he said as if he were being generous. "Your sister and my brother are flying in this afternoon."

It took a moment for his words to register, and then she had to play them back in her mind a few times before they sunk in.

"Savs and Ashton are coming here?" she asked.

"Yep, they will land in three hours."

He looked so proud of himself. And for a moment, Lexie forgot how angry she was at this man and forgot she wasn't supposed to touch him. She jumped from her chair, the ice forgotten, as she threw her arms around his neck.

She hadn't realized how much she needed her sister until he said she would soon be there. She hadn't been calling Savvy while she'd been there, just sending her short messages telling her she was fine. There was a large time difference between the Philippines and US, and she'd been worried she'd dial her in the middle of the night or interrupt something. Plus she hadn't really known what she'd say.

But when the two of them were together, everything was so easy. It was great to have a best friend who was also your sibling.

"Thank you, Lance, thank you," she said as she squeezed him.

It took several moments before she realized what she was doing, and she instantly tried to pull back, but that's when his arms came around her and swept her off her feet, landing her squarely on his lap.

"If you really want to thank me . . ." he said with a waggle of his brows.

She was so happy her sister was on the way, she actually laughed at his pathetic attempt at flirting.

"Let me go, you overgrown ape. I have things to do to prepare for my sister," she said while wiggling to get up.

He didn't release her, but the more she wiggled the more she felt him pressing into her leg. She suddenly stopped all movement and their gazes locked together.

"You're killing me, woman. I think you should know that," he said in a husky whisper as he pressed upward, letting her feel exactly what he meant.

Lexie's core instantly heated as she got lost in his eyes. It would be so easy to lean forward and accept what he wanted to give her. It would feel wonderful and take away all the ache she'd been feeling for weeks. But it was the after she was worried about.

She wanted him something fierce, but there was much more to it than desire. And that was the only thing holding her back from taking exactly what she wanted.

"Where are they staying?" she asked.

"We could bunk together and give them my room," he suggested. His hot breath washed over her, and she found the word yes resting easily on her tongue. She bit down to keep from saying it.

"That's not gonna happen," she said instead.

"Too bad," he murmured. "I guess they will stay at the hotel on the beach then. Maybe we can join them for a night. There are many romantic places we could visit," he added with a waggle of his brows.

The man was irresistible when he was happy, but when he flirted, he was a threat to society and should come with his own warning label. He wasn't going to make this easy on her at all, and she almost didn't want him to. She wanted to give in so badly it was eating her up.

"I need to get ready if we're going to the airport to get them," she told him.

He ran his hand through her hair and tugged her forward, placing a whisper-soft kiss against her lips that wasn't nearly enough. When he released her she leaned back, and his eyes were on fire. She felt the burn all the way to her core.

"You will stop fighting me one of these days, Ms. Mills," he mumbled before giving her one more quick kiss on the corner of her mouth.

On shaking knees, Lexie stood up and walked to her bedroom. She barely made it to her bed before collapsing and gazing up at the ceiling. She had a feeling he was exactly right. She only hoped she survived, if and when, she caved into the desire they both shared so strongly.

CHAPTER NINE

L ANCE NEARLY DROPPED the crate of supplies when Ashton punched him in the arm. Turning, he glared at his brother before moving the box to a table where people were in line for the new shipment.

"What in the hell was that for?" Lance asked. He wasn't going to admit the punch had actually hurt a little.

"I've missed ya. What can I say?" Ashton told him with a laugh.

"Same goes for you. Maybe I should repay the punch," Lance threatened.

"You could try, but you'd have to catch me first," Ashton said as he easily side-stepped the swing Lance sent his way. The two of them laughed as they stopped the macho posturing and returned to the truck to unload more supplies.

They made several trips before laughter caught their attention, and they both turned to look at Lexie and Savannah, sitting down with a group of children circling them as they read a story, both women getting into character and making funny noises that had the children giggling.

"Damn, did I get lucky when I married that woman," Ashton said with reverence.

"Yeah, I can't believe she fell for your sorry ass," Lance told his brother.

"Hey, it didn't have anything to do with luck. I'm one hell of a charming guy," Ashton said.

Their baby was sound asleep in the carrier next to Savvy, and Lance noticed Lexie gazed at her niece every few seconds. Seeing the woman he liked that close to a baby put thoughts in his head he didn't want to have.

"What's it like being a dad?" Lance asked, before wanting to kick himself for spurting out the first thought in his mind.

"It's exhausting," Ashton said with a smile. "And absolutely amazing."

There was no joking in his tone as he said the words, just pure awe. Lance wondered if he would ever feel that way. At the moment he couldn't imagine it. Yes, he could see never wanting to let Lexie go, but at the same time, the actual commitment of marriage and babies was too terrifying to contemplate.

"When are you going to get on with life and grow up?" Ashton asked.

The two men were done unloading, so they headed over to the tent where food and refreshments were waiting. Both grabbed a bottle of water and chugged it down.

"I would have said never a few months ago," he told Ashton honestly. That stopped his brother in his tracks as he gave Lance a look that made him want to squirm on his feet.

"Someone caught your eye?" Ashton pointedly asked as he gazed across the distance at the two women who seemed to be in heaven doing what they were doing.

"I think I'm falling for her, like *really* falling," Lance admitted. He gave up on trying to filter his thought process before speaking.

"Or it could be just great sex," Ashton told him. "Men have been known to confuse the two."

Lance thought about his brother's words for a few moments before he spoke again. He was feeling things he didn't know how to explain, and he needed someone to talk to. He certainly wasn't going to fess up to his meddling father or his recently acquired uncles. Those men always had an agenda, and if they knew what he was feeling, he'd be hearing wedding bells far before he was ready.

"We aren't having sex," Lance admitted. He wanted to bite his tongue, but at the same time it felt good to speak about important situations happening in his life with someone he trusted.

Ashton gave him an almost pitying look that made Lance want to return that punch his brother had given him earlier. Maybe he shouldn't have opened his big mouth.

"Damn, Lance, maybe you really are falling for the girl," Ashton said in awe. "If you aren't sleeping together, this is a new record for you, being with a woman *without* a happy ending."

"She's not like that," Lance snapped. He didn't appreciate his brother speaking about Lexie that way.

"Hey!" Ashton said, holding up his hands. "I wasn't implying that at all. I'm just saying if you have feelings for this woman and it doesn't stem from sex, then maybe you should hold on to her."

"She doesn't want me to," Lance said with frustration.

Ashton gave him an incredulous look before his lips twitched, and then he was outright laughing. Unable to hold back, Lance delivered that blow his brother had coming to him. But even that didn't stop the laughter from spilling out of Ashton's mouth.

"I'm not going to tell you anything ever again if you don't stop now," Lance threatened.

"I'm sorry, but you know I went through hell with Savvy. I find it fitting that you're going through something similar with her little sister," Ashton told him. "What's the problem?"

"I don't know. We had incredible sex the night of your wedding. I mean, like the best sex of my entire life, and then when I woke up the next morning she was gone, and she's been running from me ever since. Then we got here, and we have had more than one spark, but she withdraws. I can't get her to let go of the iron suit she puts on every time she's in my presence."

"Maybe she doesn't like you. Maybe the sex wasn't all that great for her," Ashton pointed out.

"No, of course not," Lance said with an eye roll. "Trust me, I know when a woman is pleased, and she was *pleased* repeatedly."

"Okay, spare me the details. She babysits my kid," Ashton said with another chuckle.

"Chemistry isn't our problem. There's something else, and I haven't quite figured out what it is."

"Here's a thought," Ashton said with another laugh. "Why don't you ask her?"

"I'm not an idiot, Ash; I've tried talking to her. She avoids anything to do with a conversation that begins with the word *we*. She's afraid of something, I'm just not sure exactly what it is."

"You know about her dad, right?" Ashton asked, all humor gone.

"No, what about him?" Lance asked, instantly attentive.

"He was an abusive asshole. He came to see Savvy once, and I ended up knocking the guy out. It took her some time, but she eventually shared with me. Maybe that's why Lexie is afraid. She was raised by a man who had no business raising kids."

"Damn. I can't imagine that. After Mom was gone, Dad wasn't quite the same, but I can admit now he did the best he could with the grief he was going through."

"Yeah, none of us were the same," Ashton pointed out. "But I finally feel as if my life has come around, as if I've gained a new purpose."

"I never thought I would want to settle down, but I look at this woman and I can't see a future without her in it," Lance admitted.

"Then it would be wise to not let her get away," Ashton told him.

"That might be some good advice."

The two men were silent as they stood there and gazed at the women they loved. It was a different life from what they'd had a couple of years ago. Maybe Lance finally *was* growing up. He didn't seem to know which way was up or down anymore, let alone how to make decisions about his future.

What he did know was that he couldn't let Lexie go without a fight. She was worth taking risks.

CHAPTER TEN

LEXIE WAS FIGHTING tears as she and Lance returned from the airport. Her sister had stayed only a few days before she and Ashton had to go back, and after having her there to lean on, Lexie was more than ready to go home too.

Maybe a month had been too long to stay. She was in a beautiful area doing amazing things, but with her thoughts all askew and her hormones going crazy, she'd rather be inside her small apartment with rain streaming down the windows, than in a shared house with Lance.

He stopped in an unfamiliar place and put the car in park before taking the keys out and turning to look at her.

"Let's go for a walk. You need cheering up," he said as he opened his door. He got out and ran around to her side, opening her door before she'd undone her seat belt.

"I'd rather go back to the house," she told him. There was so much weighing on her mind she didn't know what to do.

"Humor me," he insisted as he reached over and unclicked her belt.

The feel of his fingers sliding across her thighs whisked away her sad thoughts, and replaced them with ones she didn't want to be thinking about. She decided a walk would do her good, so she accepted his hand and stepped from the car.

They were at a beach and the sun was beginning to lower in the sky, making the view spectacular. She didn't see any other people around and wondered where he'd taken her. It was somewhere new.

They were both silent as they moved down a cleared path until they were on the sand. Lance knelt and undid her shoes, which made her smile. She kicked out of them and took off her socks then bent to lift them.

"They'll be fine here," he told her as he left his shoes next to hers.

"Okay." The two began walking, and when he reached out and took her fingers with his own, she didn't fight him. She was so tired of fighting her need to touch him, to be touched by him, and to just wrap herself around him.

Without much thought, she scooted a bit closer to him, and his fingers let hers go, which made her feel empty for a moment before his arm wrapped around her shoulders, and he pulled her in tightly to his side as they strolled leisurely along the beautiful beach.

"I will miss it here," she admitted. "But after seeing my sister, I have to admit I'm getting a little homesick."

"Yeah, I don't usually leave for this long either, but we wanted to get a lot done before Christmas, so I decided to do it all in one trip instead of two."

"What you do is pretty spectacular," she told him. "I'm glad you chose me to come along and help."

"That was an easy choice," he said.

His fingers were rubbing against her shoulder, and while the desire was always present when she was close to him, she also felt comforted and protected. Lexie was terrified because the more time she spent with this man, the more she realized she was falling for him, falling in a way that was truly going to break her in half if she wasn't careful.

"We only have a bit over a week left," she said.

"Come back again next year," he offered. She was tempted to do that. But she also knew that when they returned to Washington, the real world would settle in, she'd resume her regular life, and this would seem like nothing more than a dream.

"I was between jobs for this trip. It won't always be so easy," she told him. For some reason she wasn't ready to tell him no, but she had to prepare herself. They only had a short time left, and her defenses were down. Maybe she really did need to let go for at least a night, or maybe even a week. What would it hurt?

She stopped walking and Lance looked at her quizzically. Her heart raced as she tried to decide if she had the courage to say what she wanted to say. Awareness flashed through his eyes and she knew she was easier to read than she'd thought.

"I want you more than I can say, but I need to know you are sure," he said without her saying a single thing.

He turned her so she was facing him, his hands splayed on her back as he rubbed them up and down, going lower with each pass.

"I'm sure," she said, aching to feel his lips against hers.

He hesitated only a second longer and then closed the small distance between them as he captured her lips. She knew right then she'd made the right decision. His kiss was full of hunger as he pulled her tightly to him, his arousal pressing into the softness of her stomach, making her stand on her toes to feel him where she wanted him most.

It was too much and not nearly enough. She forgot they were on the beach, forgot about anything but him and the magic he could bring her in a way she wanted badly. She was done fighting her desperate ache for him.

His hand sifted through her hair and he tugged it hard, making her head fall back as he kissed her deeply. His demand grew as his kiss became more ardent. They'd both wanted this for so long, neither of them felt they could wait a minute more.

Sensations washed through her, and he pulled back long enough for her to take a gasping breath before crushing her mouth again and again, diving inside and claiming her as his own. And, oh how she wanted to be claimed, but only by this man in this moment.

Her body was on fire as his tongue dove inside her waiting mouth before retreating and tracing the edges of her lips. She was hungry, yearning, and couldn't get close enough to this perfect man.

Lexie didn't realize they were moving until he sat down on an outcrop of rocks, quickly tugging her into his lap, her legs wide open, her hot core perfectly positioned over his thickness. She pushed down against him, needing to feel the power of his desire. She wanted to rip clothes away from each of them and have him surge upward, deep inside her.

Even the air around them was charged. She reached behind him, grabbing his hair and pulling as she cradled him close to her. They were pressed tightly together, and it still wasn't enough. She wanted him buried so deep inside her they were truly one person. She'd heard people say that before, but she'd never felt it like she did with this man.

Lance was consuming her, and she didn't want to feel anything but his touch, anything but the desire he was giving her. She'd waited too long, and now she was ready to be his — and only his.

Pulling back, Lexie tried to follow him, but his hand slid below the hem of her shirt, and she knew his intention and was more than willing to let him go there. The last time he'd kissed her like this, he'd given her an orgasm just from his mouth on her nipples.

As hot as she was at this very moment, she had a feeling he could do it again . . . and again . . . and *please* yes . . . again.

His fingers reached her breasts, and he cupped them in his large hands, squeezing and kneading until she was whimpering against his mouth. Perfect, it was so damn perfect, she couldn't imagine anything better. Her nipples strained against his palms as she desperately sought sweet relief.

His mouth opened wider over hers, his tongue claiming her as his, and she was more than happy with the surrender. She reached between their bodies, desperately seeking his pants so she could undo them, push them away, and have him buried deep inside her. If only she'd decided to wear a skirt, it could happen that much sooner.

All Lexie wanted was for him to claim her, to make her his, to do whatever he wanted with her body. He was an incredible lover, and the places he could take her would make her journey back to reality smoother. Maybe she could live in this fantasyland longer and make it all worth it.

"I need to be buried inside you," Lance said.

"Yes, yes, please," she huskily whispered. His kiss grew more urgent as he reached for her pants.

It took a moment as lost as she was in his arms, but through the lust-filled haze of her sanity, Lexie realized Lance had stiffened beneath her, realized he'd pulled his lips from hers, and he wasn't kissing her neck, wasn't pulling off her shirt. She wanted to drag him back to her, but she felt something — something that had nothing to do with pleasure.

"You two obviously aren't lost kids. You might want to take it down a few notches, considering you're on a public beach."

The words came to Lexie through a long tunnel, or what seemed to be one. There was someone there, and by the voice, she didn't seem too happy with the activity she'd just witnessed. Lexie was so mortified she couldn't turn around. She buried her head in Lance's neck and let him face the intruder.

"I'm sorry about that. We got carried away," Lance said, putting a smile on his face that Lexie could feel even with her face buried in his neck. "We're newlyweds and can't seem to keep our hands off each other," he added.

The words sent a longing through her that she knew was wrong on so many levels. The glare she'd felt at her back disappeared though as the person spoke again, this time far less harshly.

"Oh, that's so sweet," she said. "But why don't you take it back to your room?"

"We'll do that," Lance said easily. "Have a great day."

There were several moments of utter silence and Lexie refused to remove her face from where it was buried, then she felt Lance's chest shake as he let out a laugh. She didn't see what he had to laugh about. The situation was mortifying.

"I don't think I've been caught with my pants down in a long time," he said. "The coast is clear, so you can quit hiding."

"Thankfully our pants *weren't* down," she told him, still far too mortified to be laughing about the situation.

"I plan on rectifying that as soon as I get you home," he told her. He stood up, easily carrying her in his arms. Lexie was still afraid to show her face, so she kept it right where it was, even though she was embarrassed to be carried around by this man.

"Yeah, I think the mood is over," she told him.

"I can get you back in the mood," he said, panic popping into his voice as he picked up his pace.

"This is too hard, Lance. I think we made a mistake," she said.

He stopped, and she was now afraid to look at him for fear of seeing disgust in his expression. He set her down, and she realized they'd already made it to the car. When he didn't speak for several moments she was left with no choice but to finally look at him.

"Us together is *never* a mistake," he said as he placed a gentle finger beneath her chin. "But if you want to wait a while longer, I will accept that."

She was so awed by his understanding, she wanted to throw her arms around him again and restart the unfinished kissing. But she was also confused. And with her hormones not raging, those doubts popped up in her mind again, those images of her father hitting her mother, hitting her sister.

"Can you take me home?" she asked.

He was disappointed, she could clearly see that, but he covered it up quickly. "Yes, of course. Let me run down and grab our shoes first."

Lexie was grateful for the few moments by herself as she tried to collect herself. It was growing harder for her to believe it possible for Lance to have a dark side. But that's what really frightened her. If he did ever turn on her, she would never trust a single soul again.

Lance reached over on the drive back and placed his hand on her leg. This time it wasn't about sex; it was about comfort. He was telling her without words that he was there for her. She was a fool to not take what he was offering. A big fool.

CHAPTER ELEVEN

L EXIE LOOKED AT the jet as she and Lance made their way to it. Her only thought was that she'd been a fool. More than a week ago she'd been ready to make love to him, but she'd been scared, and by the time they'd returned to the house, she had decided it wasn't worth the risk of losing her heart to him.

She'd already given him a piece of her and now it was too late. Their trip was going to be over soon, and she'd be back in the real world where men like Lance Storm didn't hang out with ordinary women like her unless there was something wrong with them.

Sure, her sister had married his brother, but her sister was also a genius and going places in life. Lexie wasn't as lucky as Savs. She had wandered a long time, trying to find herself. She was now getting older, and the journey felt like it was only beginning.

They stepped into the plane and the sadness was overwhelming. She wished she was brave enough to share how she was feeling, but she knew she'd keep it all inside. If she didn't act vulnerable, she felt more protected. That might someday be her downfall.

Lance wasn't wearing his customary smile when they entered the jet, and she wanted to reach out to him, but he left her in the main part of the plane and disappeared down the hallway. Was he in the bedroom? Should she follow him? There were so many things she wanted to do, but instead she sat in the same seat she'd been in on the flight there and accepted a vodka tonic, gulping it down and asking for a second.

It didn't take long for the jet to close, and when they were taxiing down the runway, she still didn't see Lance. Maybe he'd given up on her. If she were him, she most certainly would have by now. She was rational one minute, and then tucked safely back inside her own head the next. She was acting like a crazy woman, and every person had their breaking point when dealing with someone like her.

Lexie sat by herself, feeling the weight of sadness flowing over her as they lifted into the sky and she said goodbye to another chapter in her life. She'd always admired her sister, and she wished she were there with her now.

But with only a week until Christmas, there was no way Lexie was going to burden her sister with her messy emotions. She would do what she always did and hold it inside, doing her best to make it through not only this flight, but the rest of her life back in the real world.

Lance didn't reappear, and Lexie turned away the offered meal, feeling the weight of not sleeping much settle over her. She let her eyes close.

Waking in the middle of the night, Lexie was vaguely aware of a blanket over her. Exhaustion pulled her back under as she snuggled deeper into the blanket and thanked the blissful blackness that took her sadness away.

"Lexie . . . Lexie . . ." The chipper voice was pulling her from a wonderful dream and she didn't want to wake up. Her hand fluttered as she tried to shoo the voice away.

"Come on, beautiful, it's time to wake up. You've slept for about fourteen hours straight. If I hadn't seen your chest moving, I would have been a little concerned."

"What?" The fog was lifting as Lexie opened her eyes. It took a minute for her to focus but when she did, she saw Lance leaning over her, a soft smile on his lips. He looked so different from the man she'd boarded the jet with. "Did you say I've slept for fourteen hours?"

Lexie sat up, the rest of her sleep-drugged mind clearing as she looked out the dark windows, rain sliding down them. They were no longer in the Philippines, that was for sure.

"Yep. I guess jet lag and exhaustion have finally caught up to you," he said with a chuckle.

"We're almost home?" She gasped. The rest of her time with Lance was gone, just like that. She felt closer to crying than ever before.

"Yep, we're starting our descent into Seattle," he told her.

Lexie had to keep her lips sealed because she was afraid she would burst into tears. She hadn't thought she'd be brave enough to take him back to that beautiful bedroom at the back of the jet, but now she would never know. Her little nap had turned into a full-on snooze fest.

"I'm sorry," she said, though she wasn't sure who she was apologizing to. Maybe it was to him, or maybe to herself. She'd missed an opportunity of a lifetime, and in a short time she'd be saying goodbye for good.

"Lexie, I have a favor to ask," he said. That caught her attention. After everything the man had done for her, she wasn't sure she could say no to anything he asked — especially if it was to warm his bed for the night.

Dang, her mind had sunk to the gutter and it seemed it wasn't coming up anytime soon. As soon as she was away from him, things would change. Until then, she had to keep herself together.

"Of course. What do you need?"

"A girlfriend for the week."

It took a bit to process his words. She looked at him as if he was crazy. She waited for him to go on, but he just smiled as if he was asking the most reasonable thing in the world.

"Did you say a girlfriend — like a middle school fling?" she asked, needing to make sure she'd heard what she thought she had.

"Yep, exactly. Want to help a guy out?" He still wore that innocent expression, and she didn't know what to think.

"I don't understand what you're asking," she told him.

He smiled that smile that made her want to do anything he wanted. It was a killer grin, and she could see it getting her into more trouble than she cared to get into.

"My family is putting on pressure this year for me to settle down and get married. If I take you to the lodge for the holiday, maybe they will lay off. They know we just spent a month together, so they wouldn't blink at a romance blossoming. Come with me for a messy, crazy, chaotic Christmas and act like I'm irresistible to you, and I will be your servant for life," he told her.

Lexie's first thought was to tell him she wouldn't mind being his real girlfriend. Luckily she stopped before saying that out loud. Her next thought was there was no way she would be able to pull that off. She wasn't an actress. But as she looked at him, she realized she wouldn't be putting on much of an act at all. She *had* been falling for the guy. To pretend she was doing exactly that would be easy. And she wouldn't need to have her heart broken, because he would assume it was all an act and wouldn't know how she truly felt. But she couldn't just crash a family Christmas, could she?

"I don't think that sounds like a very good idea," she told him.

His expression didn't falter. "Come on, Lex, there will be turkey and ham, mashed potatoes and yams, all the treats you can imagine, *and* your sister will be there," he added as if the rest wasn't tempting enough.

"Savvy will know it's an act," she pointed out. "I've never been able to lie to her."

"We'll bring her in on the secret if it becomes necessary," he said as if it were a done deal. "What were you going to do anyway?"

Lexie didn't want to admit what her Christmas plans had been. They were too pathetic to talk about. Of course, Savs had tried to get her to come to the holiday bash he was speaking of, but she'd made excuses not to. Now that Lance was inviting her, the temptation to go was so great she didn't want to say no. She found herself gazing at him, wondering if her silent tears had been so obvious he was making this up because he felt sorry for her.

"What exactly would I have to do?" she asked. She couldn't believe she was actually considering this.

"You just have to laugh at my dumb jokes, pretend you can't live without me, and say only great things to my family about what a wonderful guy I am," he said with a wink.

"I think that's impossible," she told him with a roll of her eyes.

"Ah, come on, you had fun with me over the last month, didn't you?"

"It wasn't *all* bad," she admitted.

"That's the spirit," he told her with that mesmerizing smile. "So tell me you'll come, so I don't have to kidnap you," he insisted.

"Okay."

Lexie wasn't sure which of them was more shocked when she said that one simple word. Her gaze widened as they looked into each other's eyes, and she felt him lean in just a little and wondered if he wanted to seal the deal with a kiss.

She'd have to continue to wonder, because the captain announced they had to buckle up for landing in a few minutes. Lexie glanced over at Lance as they touched down and wondered if she should take back her agreement.

But as she tried to utter the words, she realized she didn't want to. The last thing she wanted was to leave the airport and go to an empty apartment with no Christmas decorations and nothing but loneliness.

At least for this holiday season she could pretend her life was golden, and she'd be doing it on the arm of Lance Storm. Her life could be a hell of a lot worse right now.

CHAPTER TWELVE

L ANCE DIDN'T UNDERSTAND why he was so damn nervous. He'd spent the last month with this woman who was now quietly riding next to him, looking out the window as they climbed higher into the mountains. The snow appeared to be turning into a blizzard.

His family was one of those rare entities that enjoyed the holidays, and even more strangely, enjoyed each other's company. It hadn't been that way for a lot of years, but since meeting new relatives they hadn't known they had, their family had tripled, and now any occasion to get together was worth celebrating.

Lance's uncle Joseph had bought a lodge in the mountains of Washington and that was where the family spent Christmas every year now. Lance wasn't sure how many rooms were in the place, but he knew it had once been a travel destination. A person could seriously get lost while trying to find the kitchen if they weren't careful.

The closer they drew to the lodge, the more excited Lance became. He was going there with Lexie as his girlfriend, and by the end of the visit, he hoped and prayed it was true. Yes, he also wanted to make love to her more than he wanted to keep his legs attached and he couldn't stomach the thought of letting her go.

For most of the return flight, he'd gazed at this woman who had changed his entire way of thinking. He had to find out if it was her father's abuse that she was so afraid of. If she decided to share with him, maybe the two of them could begin to build some sort of future together.

Far too soon, he was pulling up to the lodge where a dozen vehicles were getting buried in the falling snow. It looked as if they were the last to arrive. He looked at the lights glistening around the lodge. This year his father and uncles had gone all out.

He smiled knowing his brothers and cousins had been out there freezing their butts off as they hooked them all up. The females would have gotten a pass since they'd taken over cooking for the huge clan. Except for Christmas Eve and Day. His uncles and father brought in cooks so the family could enjoy each other fully on those magical days.

If he'd been a day sooner, he would have been risking life and limb to hang whatever the patriarchs of the family had demanded. It seemed like the decorations got a bit crazier every year.

Lexie gazed in awe at the sight before she faced him with a panicked look on her beautiful face. It was too late for her to back out, so he wasn't worried about it.

"This looks like a storefront," she said, obviously wondering if they were in the correct place.

"Yep, that would be Uncle Joseph and Uncle George's fault, along with my father, Richard," Lance said with a chuckle.

"I thought you said we were going to a house," she said, looking a bit distrustful.

"Well, it's a large family so Uncle Joseph *considers* this a house," he said before he stepped from the car and ran around to open her door. Lance loved that she waited for him. It was such a simple thing, but he liked opening her door, pulling out her chair, and holding her hand. It made him feel like he was taking care of her.

"We can stand here in the snow and make out in case anyone is peeking through the windows," he suggested.

Lexie gave him an eye roll before she turned back to the lodge. "Let's save the acting for when we know people are watching," she said.

"Who said it was acting?" he asked as he pushed her against the car and brushed some hair out of her face. He needed another taste of her, and being at this place made him realize he would be expected to kiss her all he wanted. He should have brought the two of them to his family a heck of a lot sooner.

"Lance . . ." He wasn't sure if it was a protest or a come-on, but the way his name rushed off her lips in that husky voice made him hard and ready in less than a second. Hell with the acting, he wanted to take her right there against the side of the car that was getting buried in snow. They were both hot enough it would all melt around them anyway.

Leaning in, he took her lips, the snow encasing them. She was tense for less than a second before she reached for him and kissed him back with the same pent-up passion they'd been suppressing for too long.

"Hey everyone, it looks like Lance has finally decided to bless us with his presence. Of course he seems to be a little distracted right now, busy in the front yard."

The voice carried over to them from the front of the lodge. Lance broke away with a growl. Why did he continue kissing her where it was bound to end badly for him just when it was time for the good stuff to start?

He looked up to find the front porch of the lodge filling up with various family members, all of them smiling at him and Lexie, who once again looked a bit mortified.

"Remember, you're my girlfriend and this is natural," he whispered in her ear before letting her go and sliding his fingers into hers.

Uncle Joseph didn't miss the hand-holding. Lance was counting on that. If he thought Lance was happy, then Lance might make it through a single holiday without being grilled on when he was going to take a walk down the aisle. Sooner than everyone might think if he didn't manage to clear his head.

"Hello, Uncle Joseph," he said before pausing and looking around at the rest of the group, who were all eyeing Lexie. "And gang," he added with a chuckle, "you all know Lexie, she's Savs's little sister. We just returned from our trip."

Lexie wasn't saying anything, but he did notice how she snuggled closer against his side. He would like to think it was because she couldn't keep her hands off him, but in reality he knew it was because his family was damn intimidating.

"About time you brought a beautiful woman home with you." This time the words came from Uncle George.

"I thought you'd like that since I haven't managed to do any Christmas shopping yet," Lance said with a chuckle.

"Let's get inside before we freeze to death," said his father, Richard, the only one who seemed to be reasonable.

The second they stepped into the house, chaos was a surety. He could hear his nieces and nephews playing as they ran around and the chatter from many couples as they made their way through the lodge to the giant living room that miraculously fit them all.

"It's so good to see you again, Lexie," Joseph said as he pushed his way in and grabbed her before she knew what was happening.

Lance's eyes met hers when Joseph set her back on the ground, and yes, he saw a little panic in her gaze, but he also saw wonder. Lance couldn't look away as he watched a suspicious sparkle appear in her eyes before she managed to push it down. Their gazes connected, and he was lost in the little girl he saw hidden beneath the tough demeanor. She wanted to be a part of a family. She was so afraid of being hurt, but she did a damn good job of hiding how she truly felt.

He hadn't thought about that before. Maybe he needed to approach her from a whole new perspective, let her know he had no intentions of walking away from her. Maybe he needed to assure himself that he wasn't going anywhere. Maybe it was time he stopped pretending he was so great on his own.

"I'm sorry to barge in and interrupt your Christmas," Lexie said as Joseph looked at her.

"Nonsense, my dear," Joseph said with a brush of his hand in the air. "The fuller this place becomes, the happier I am."

"Thank you," Lexie said, her voice choked with emotion.

Lance couldn't stand not to comfort her. He slipped in beside her and wrapped her next to him as he addressed his uncle.

"I know Lexie being here is like me bringing in a shiny new toy for you all to play with and quiz, but let's give her a break for now," he said.

His uncle looked at him in surprise, making him realize he'd sounded a bit more possessive than he'd intended. He wanted them to think she was his girl, but he didn't want their match-making antics to step up on the ladder. Sure, he was processing in his own mind not wanting to let this woman go, but it needed to be his idea, not the meddlers'.

"Well said, my boy," Joseph boomed, making Lexie squeeze in tighter to his side.

"Where's my sister?" Lexie asked.

"She and Ashton ran into town. They should be home soon," George told her.

"Good, now everyone can get to know each other over the next few days. We don't need a barrage of introductions immediately," Lance said. "We came straight from the airport, and we're tired."

"Do you want to head to your room now?" Joseph asked with too much enthusiasm.

"I think we could use some food," Lance told him with a grin. Of course, if Lexie was willing, he'd be more than happy to satisfy his other appetite that wouldn't go away. He wasn't going to say that to his family though.

"Of course. How rude of us," George said. "Why don't we take your bags up to your room so you can settle in later?"

"I can get the bags with the help of a couple cousins. Lexie doesn't pack light," he said with a laugh.

"Well, of course not, boy. You guys were gone a full month," Joseph admonished him. He laughed, but was glad when his uncle turned to leave.

The room cleared out, leaving Lexie standing by his side. He was thinking he might have asked for too much, bringing her to this chaotic place his family liked to call a vacation.

"Do you want to run away?" he asked her, terrified she would say yes. She'd barely gotten an inquisition, and they'd been there for ten minutes. It was going to get worse, although he didn't want to tell her that.

"I think I might adore your family," she said shyly, knocking him back a step or two as he gazed at her.

"And I think I might be liking you, Ms. Mills," he said.

He once again got lost in her gaze, but Lance wasn't a fool. The next time he kissed her, it was damn well going to be somewhere they wouldn't get interrupted.

CHAPTER THIRTEEN

L EXIE FELT AS if she were in an entirely different universe. This mansion they called a lodge had so much space, but she still felt locked in. So many gazes were upon her and the laughter and chatter wasn't something she was used to. In her small universe, family meant her and her sister.

With the Anderson-Storm clan, family was endless. There were cousins, uncles, aunts, siblings. It went on and on and on, and she was afraid to get attached to the atmosphere. She watched as these incredibly wealthy, but still normal, people opened their hearts to her sister as if she'd been with them all her life.

It was everything Lexie had dreamed about when she was younger, but hadn't dared hope would come true. She had to keep telling herself she was simply a guest. She was there because Lance didn't want his family to keep pushing him to get married. She was his fake girlfriend for the holidays.

If she began to hope for it to be real, she would be lost. She couldn't do that to herself. This was her sister's world — Lance's world. It wasn't hers. But sitting next to Lance at the enormous table, as family members passed around the roast, potatoes, and so many sides she didn't see how all the food would get eaten, drew her in.

The outside of the house looked like an airport where she might be waiting for the CEO's helicopter to land at any moment. But the inside was just as outrageous. There wasn't only one tree set up, but four, with bright, colorful lights and ornaments in all shapes and sizes, including ones the grandkids had carefully made and hung in all different places, adding to its charm.

With the snow falling outside, she felt like she'd stepped into a Hallmark movie — one she never wanted to end. Lexie hadn't had much of an appetite for a full week, but soon she was stuffed as she continued to feed her face, which was better than answering the millions of questions shot her way.

"I'm so glad you two found love while serving others," Joseph said from the head of the table, his voice easily carrying down to her, as well as to the other end, where his brother George sat.

"Me too," Lance agreed quickly, saving her from having to answer. If they quizzed her, asked her if she loved Lance, she realized it wouldn't be a lie if she said yes.

Lexie feared Lance would hear the truth in her words though, and then he would feel sorry for her, or run for his life. He hadn't asked her to be his for life, he'd asked her to pretend to be his. Yes, she knew he wouldn't mind some bonus sex. For that matter, she wouldn't either. But if she took this fantasy too far . . .

Shaking her head, she stopped her train of thought. She knew all the reasons she needed to pull back from Lance, but at the same time, she also needed to put on a convincing act and earn her place at the Anderson family extravaganza.

Lance laughed next to her, and Lexie took the opportunity to study him. He was not the type she'd gone after before. Not that she'd been on the hunt for men. She'd been busy with other pursuits.

But he was handsome to the point of being scary. Women would always hit on him with his dark hair, sparkling eyes, and square jaw. He even had perfect laugh lines around his eyes that spoke of happiness in his life. There was a rugged sexiness to him when he didn't shave for a few days. He was too much for her to hold on to, even if he wanted or thought he wanted her to.

Lexie had always been sure of herself. She could look in the mirror and be happy with the image that greeted her. She took care of herself, washed and lotioned her face, worked out, and was conscious of how she appeared. But she wasn't vain. There were many prettier women out there . . . and hungrier. They would consider Lance a real catch, so if she wasn't willing to reel him in, they certainly would be.

Lexie was so intent on studying Lance, she jumped when he reached out and pushed her hair back from her face, his intense eyes focused on her. There was a question in them she didn't know how to answer, so she smiled, trying to reassure him that everything was fine — she was fine.

But Lexie wasn't fine. She was terrified and wanted to run and hide. She didn't see that happening anytime soon. As Lance touched her, she felt her insides stir, felt a deep connection with him she couldn't push down. She forgot they were surrounded by his family.

She wanted desperately to lean into him, feel assured by his touch, and tell him to take her for now or for always. But Lexie was better at controlling her emotions and feelings, and she did none of that.

"Are you okay?" Lance asked quietly for her ears only.

"This is a bit overwhelming," she admitted.

"My family is slightly insane, but they are good people," he told her.

"I can see that," she said.

It was just the two of them in their own little bubble, and she liked that as much as she liked being with his ginormous family. That urge to lean into him, to accept the offer in his eyes, was growing stronger by the minute.

"What are you two whispering about?" a voice asked.

It took a moment for Lexie to realize the question was addressed to her and Lance. She jerked her gaze away from him, feeling her cheeks heat as she looked around and noticed most of the family looking in their direction — including her sister who had a pleased smile on her face. Lexie gave her a look that didn't need words, but that only made Savvy smile that much more.

"We were just talking about how long a day it's been," Lance said, quickly saving her. His hand reached beneath the table and rested on her thigh to give her a reassuring squeeze.

She was sure he had meant well by doing so, but his touch made her burn in a way she didn't want to in front of his entire family. They'd lasted a month sharing a place with very little sexual interaction. That wasn't doing her any good at the moment, because she wanted him so desperately she wished they were snowed-in at some cabin far away from society.

Instead of moving his hand away, his fingers splayed wide, his pinkie coming far too close to her neglected parts. She began taking shallow breaths, hoping not to pass out or moan, or both.

Lexie wasn't even sure if Lance was aware of his fingers rubbing little patterns on the denim of her jeans, but she might as well have been naked for all the protection her clothes were giving her. Her skin was heating, and she wanted desperately to end this family dinner.

But that meant she would be going to a room she was sharing with Lance. When she'd found out they'd been put in the same one, she'd wanted to protest. Her will wasn't that strong. But she would have blown their cover if she'd done that, so she'd said nothing.

And as much as she was afraid to go to that room with him, she was almost more afraid of sitting at a table with his family and falling more in love with all of them by the second.

This was going to be a very long week, she decided. She might end up in a mental institution at the end of it, if she survived in the first place. Thank goodness her sister was there. But with so many people around, Lexie didn't know if she'd be able to pull her sister away to have a heart-to-heart talk.

"Of course you're tired. Why don't you go on up and get some rest? We have a lot of activities planned over the next few days," Joseph said.

A few people stood as everyone agreed it was late and time to turn in. Lexie watched in fascination as some of the couples who had been married for years looked at each other with hunger. She didn't understand how their passion and love for each other had withstood so much time, but she was beginning to think love was possible with the right person.

"Shouldn't we help clean up first?" Lexie asked when Lance stood and held out a hand to her.

"It's all taken care of, dear. You go get some rest," George told her.

Reluctantly, Lexie allowed Lance to pull her away. They made it to the large doorway leading away from the dining area when a chorus of yells called them to a stop.

"What?" she asked with panic as she looked around. Had she done something wrong? Was the house on fire? But as she looked at the faces smiling back at her she feared it might be something worse. She was right.

"Look up," Savvy, her traitorous sister, called out in a sing-song voice.

Lexie was afraid to do just that, but she did, and then glared at the huge clump of mistletoe hanging from the arch. She then looked at Lance who was grinning at her.

"You can't pass under it without a kiss," Lucas called out. He was Lance's oldest cousin. She wanted to point out to him that he had a teenage daughter, and she was sure he wouldn't be enforcing the rules if Jasmine were to walk under the mistletoe with some boy. But she bit her tongue and didn't say anything.

"We wouldn't want to miss out on a holiday tradition," Lance said with a chuckle as he pulled her close. Lexie gazed into his eyes feeling lost, her body trembling.

"We can't kiss in front of your entire family," she whispered.

"Ah, it will just be a little kiss," he assured her.

It would be a little kiss and then they would be traipsing up a bunch of stairs and closing themselves in a room together. Lexie wondered how much she could handle before she completely lost it.

"When you lick your lips like that it drives me insane," Lance told her. Lexie hadn't even realized her tongue had exited her mouth. But she sucked it inside quickly as she continued to look into his sparkling eyes.

"The damage is done," he told her. "But when we're in private you can use that tongue however you'd like."

Lexie's core tightened as her body sizzled in anticipation. Maybe she should give in to the desire humming between them. They were both adults, both responsible. Why couldn't she loosen the reins on herself and let it go? It would be so easy to do with this particular man.

As she continued looking at him, she heard a chant behind them. *Kiss, kiss, kiss . . .*

"We better do what the crowd is demanding or there could be a riot," Lance told her.

Then he stopped talking and took over, a much wiser course of action. Reaching up, he cupped her face, then quickly closed the distance between them. The first kiss was soft and gentle, more a brushing of lips than a connection. It was enough to send a shiver all the way down her spine.

The next touch was a bit rougher with his lips connecting and not releasing from hers. His hand shifted behind her neck and held her in place as he coaxed her mouth open for his tongue.

With a sigh, Lexie forgot about his family and her sister sitting behind them, watching this incredibly intimate moment. She forgot about why she shouldn't be kissing this man at all. She reached for him, her hands winding behind his neck as she held on and enjoyed the passion he brought out in her.

His tongue slowly passed into her mouth as he tangled it with her own, and the burn inside her body ignited, threatened to singe her right there. She clung tighter to him as he played her mouth as expertly as he'd played her body earlier.

When she heard a cheer go up Lexie realize their kiss was getting out of control. Her body was molded against Lance's and her skin was flushed. Mortified, she buried her face against Lance's neck as he turned to address his family.

"Go away," he said with a growl. "Better yet, *we're* going away," he told them. Laughter followed his words.

Lexie didn't look up as Lance turned them and practically ran away to shouts from his brothers. Lexie didn't want to focus on what they were shouting to the two of them. She was too embarrassed to speak at the moment. She was shocked her legs were working at all.

The lodge was so big that it took a little while to get to their bedroom. But when he opened the door and she stepped through, she felt like a fly entering the spider's den. She was in trouble — real trouble.

CHAPTER FOURTEEN

L ANCE HAD SWORN not to kiss Lexie again if he wouldn't be able to finish what that would start. He'd failed on that promise to himself in only a few hours' time. The moment his lips had connected with Lexie's he'd been lost. He hadn't cared where they were, he'd only cared about getting her to a bed, or a wall. Hell, the floor would have worked.

He wanted this woman with a passion he was sure was going to kill him. He didn't care. If he died in her arms, it would be a happy death. But please, he prayed to the heavens, let him have a release first.

The look on Lexie's face as they entered the large bedroom wasn't reassuring him that he was going to get that happy night today. She was protecting herself, but he didn't understand from what. He wasn't a terrible guy, and the two of them had chemistry. Hell, they had more than chemistry — they had something that was both amazing and terrifying. But at least he was willing to explore it. He didn't think she was. It had to do with her father, he decided.

Lance had pushed her into coming to stay with his family, and now he wondered if that had been a mistake. Maybe she was so overwhelmed she'd go running off to the hills, never to be found again. It was done, though, and there was nothing he could do to change it, so he might as well try to make the best of the situation.

"Your family is . . . a lot to take in," Lexie finally said as she wandered around the room. He noticed she didn't go anywhere near the bed.

Someone had come up earlier and turned on the gas fireplace, the glow from the lamp and the fire the only light in the room. If he couldn't seduce her in this room, all hope was lost.

"Yeah, it took time to get used to it," he admitted.

"What do you mean?" she asked.

"Didn't your sister fill you in?" he questioned.

"Not really. She just says she loves them all," she told him. "I can completely understand why. They are wonderful."

Of course Savvy loved his family. Once a person got to know them, it was impossible not to want to be a part of the Anderson clan.

"My dad was a triplet, but he didn't know," Lance began to explain. "The doctor who delivered them discovered a third baby, and since he and his wife couldn't have children, they decided it was fate. So Joseph and George grew up with their parents never knowing about my dad. About six years ago, my dad decided to move from the East Coast to Seattle and that's when they all met. My siblings and I discovered we had a hoard of cousins and they took us right in. It was a bit of an adjustment, but now we're as close as if we'd never been apart," he told her.

"Wow," she said in awe, moving over to the bed and plopping down. The sight of her on that large mattress had him growing uncomfortably hard. Damn, he couldn't even have a normal conversation without sex on the brain.

"Yeah, it really is quite the story, but my family was falling apart and moving here healed us in ways I can't even begin to describe. I'm grateful to have them. And yes, they are meddling and drive me insane sometimes, but I can't image my life without them," he admitted.

"You're a good guy, Lance," she said. The words came out sounding more like an accusation than a compliment.

"Is that a bad thing?" he asked with a smile.

"No . . . and yes," she said. She suddenly appeared so sad that he wanted to walk over and comfort her. He feared if he did it would lead to other things though, and he didn't want her to think he saw her as nothing but a body to use.

Damn! He wished he had no morals. He knew there was more to the two of them than just wanting her physically, but he'd never been good at talking and sharing his feelings. He didn't want to screw this up. If only he knew what to do next.

"I'm glad you came here. No one should be alone at Christmas," he said. He moved over to his bag and began taking some things out so he could occupy his hands before he went over and filled them with her luscious assets.

"I'm used to being alone," she told him.

"That shouldn't be the case, Lexie. Your sister is married to my brother. That means you're family," he told her.

She looked at him with so much hope in her eyes he didn't know what to think. Maybe that's what he'd needed to say all along. Maybe she just needed to know she belonged somewhere. It wasn't something he'd ever dealt with before. Even when he and his siblings hadn't been on the best of terms, he'd always known he had a place to come home to. He assumed everyone felt the same.

"This is Savvy's new destiny, not mine. I've leaned on her for a long time. I have to learn to stand on my own," she told him.

"That's not true. We aren't meant to do it on our own. The people who love us never mind that we accept their help," he told her.

"Sometimes we have to grow up," she countered.

"And sometimes growing up means knowing when to ask for help," he insisted.

"You have all the answers, don't you?" she said with a chuckle.

"I'm a smart guy," he said.

"That you are," she told him. "Do you want the bathroom first?"

"No, go ahead."

Lexie grabbed some items from one of her bags and disappeared into the connecting bathroom. Lance groaned as he heard the shower turn on and pictured her peeling her clothes away and climbing inside, steam surrounding her, soap dripping down her chest, over her stomach and . . .

Whoa! He couldn't be having those thoughts. It would make it impossible for him to get any sleep regardless of how exhausted he was. He glanced at the bed again and felt an ache filter through him. He couldn't just assume she'd want to share the bed, though that would make the night a hell of a lot more pleasant.

He'd give her the choice, but he'd also be a gentleman and make a separate bed. If she wanted to invite him into her bed instead of making him sleep on the floor, he certainly wouldn't complain.

He pulled some blankets out of the closet and laid them out in front of the fire. If he wasn't going to enjoy her body heat, then he needed something to keep him warm on this cold night — not that his own body temperature wasn't scorching hot right now.

Lexie didn't take too long in the bathroom and when she came out, her peachy scent assaulted him. He wanted to take that bite out of her he'd been fantasizing about for a month. Her cheeks were glowing, and with her hair wet and hanging down her back, she looked so young and innocent that he almost felt guilty about having thoughts of her writhing beneath him.

Lance didn't trust himself to say a word, so instead he slipped into the bathroom and shut the door, the scent of her was even stronger in the closed room. Stripping down, he looked at the misbehaving part of his body and cursed how hard he was.

He stepped into the shower she'd just been naked and wet in and whimpered in pain as he pulsed. Reaching down, he squeezed himself to the point of pain, trying to make the traitorous erection die away. But that did nothing.

Placing his hands on the wall, he wondered if it was okay to let out a few tears of frustration. That thought had him smiling.

It took a lot to bring Lance to his knees, but he had a feeling the woman on the other side of the door could do it easily.

He again thought of relieving himself, but he couldn't do it, not with the chance of her doing it for him. He was saying every prayer imaginable that he would walk back into the room and see her lying on the bed with a come-hither look on her face and open arms.

Reality wasn't nearly as appealing as his fantasies. He left his shirt off, walking from the bathroom in a pair of low slung sweatpants, sweat from his hot shower gleaming on his chest.

Pride filtered through him when Lexie stopped pulling the covers back on the bed and stared at his pecs. Lance was one of the lucky ones that had a great metabolism, and it didn't take much to keep his body in shape, but he still worked out hard and didn't mind one little bit at her looking.

Her face assured him she wasn't planning on sharing the same bed. With almost a sad sigh, he moved across the room and looked at the covers he'd laid out on the floor. It was less than appealing.

"I'll sleep down here if you prefer," he told her. "But I don't mind sharing that nice big bed with you."

Lexie's eyes widened, and he saw desire flare. For one second he had hope that she was going to invite him in. He could seduce her. He knew that, but he wanted her to want him without the seduction. He wanted her to let go of her inhibitions and let him love her.

"Your entire family is on the other side of this door. There's no way I'm going to risk them hearing us doing . . . things," she finally said with that intriguing blush stealing over her features.

"They wouldn't hear a thing. It's a big place," he said. If that was all that was stopping her, he could certainly win this one.

"Good try," she said with a forced chuckle.

Then he watched in agony as she bent over, her nice tush a pleasant sight, before it disappeared as she climbed beneath the covers, pulling them all the way up to her chin.

"We could both be sleeping like puppies if you'd let me help you relax," he tried one more time. But he knew it was a losing battle. He sank to the floor, too hot to get under the blankets, so he laid on top instead, his hand beneath his head as he gazed at what an appealing sight she made, her body lost in all those covers.

The dim light of the room cast a perfect glow on her features and made him want her that much more. He had never respected a woman this much, and he sort of liked how much he did. He didn't want to do anything to dishonor Lexie.

With a sigh that sounded as pained as he felt, Lexie reached over and clicked off her bedside lamp. The glow from the fire was the only light in the room, and Lance had put the setting on low so it was only enough to cast shadows, but still he could see her face, even if he could no longer read her expression.

He feared it was going to be a very long night. The floor felt harder than normal, even though he'd slept on worse in the past. If he didn't get into her bed soon, he'd be suffering all sorts of aches and pains.

The silence weighed on Lance as he tried to get comfortable. After several minutes he wondered if she'd fallen asleep. Maybe that was best. He certainly could use a refresh session.

"Goodnight, Lance," she finally said, the words drifting lazily over to him. "Thanks for bringing me here."

His heart swelled at her words. She might be feeling overwhelmed, but she also appreciated his messy family. That tugged on his heart more than anything else that had been said or done between the two of them.

Though Lance hadn't thought he'd be able to sleep, he focused on Lexie all snug in her bed, and soon his eyes were drifting closed, her face flashing in his mind. He was falling more and more for her. And he wasn't afraid.

CHAPTER FIFTEEN

PERFECTION.

Lexie was perfect in every single way. Her hair tickled its way down his belly as her hands traced the ridges on his stomach before she tugged on his pants. He lifted his hips so she could slip the pants away, and then he felt her hot breath on his thickness, her mouth descending. He couldn't open his eyes, couldn't do anything other than enjoy the feel of her touching him — tasting him.

A groan escaped his mouth at the first swipe of her tongue down his entire length. He didn't even try to hold back the moan this time. He was pulsing in her hand as she wrapped her fingers around him. Then her mouth circled the tip of his hardness, and she tasted him and moaned, the vibration of her mouth sending him over the edge of sanity.

More. He wanted so much more than her mouth. "Lexie . . ." he groaned, reaching down for her, but coming up empty. Her magical mouth moved up and down him, and he was so close . . . so very close to releasing. But he wanted to be buried deep inside her the next time he let go so he held back.

It had been over a year since he'd felt the hot slickness of her heat surrounding him. He almost forgot what it felt like — almost, but not quite. The next time he came it was going to be because he was buried to the hilt deep within her body. Nothing else would be as satisfying.

"Lance . . ." she called again, but this time there was real urgency in her voice. He whimpered when her hot, wet mouth left his thickness. No. He wasn't ready unless she was planning on crawling up his body and sitting down on him. He was more than ready for that.

"Lance!" This time her voice was angry, and Lance didn't understand. Had he done something wrong? He didn't want to open his eyes, but he knew he needed to. Something wasn't right.

"Wake up!" Lexie hissed.

Lance's eyes flew open, and he looked down. Lexie wasn't on him, and his pants weren't down. There was certainly a tent where his erection was standing at attention, but when he realized he'd been dreaming he almost felt the sting of tears. He wasn't going to last, not at all — not like this. Maybe seduction was back on the table. He'd been an honorable man for long enough.

Lance focused on Lexie, who was sitting up in bed looking frightened, and then he heard the knock on the bedroom door. He turned in that direction. Why was she freaking out?

"Hello? It's late morning, and we have to get going. I'll wait two minutes for you two to get decent, and then I'm opening the door," a voice called through the closed door.

"Soundproof my butt," Lexie said with a glare sent his way. "Get up here on the bed with me," she demanded.

"Hell yeah," he said as he scrambled to his feet, forgetting the person at the door.

"Not for that, you fool," she snapped, making his erection twitch. "We're supposed to be a couple. Couples tend to sleep together," she hissed.

Lance wanted to go back to sleep and continue where his dream had left off. It had been much more pleasant than the reality of Lexie inviting him into bed as a showpiece instead of as her lover.

"Come on," she said urgently as he saw the knob on the door begin to turn.

Lance dove into motion, though he didn't know why he was doing so. He made it to the bed and Lexie reached for him, pulling, knocking him off balance. He slipped and fell on top of her, their eyes meeting as she lost her breath at his weight.

He'd been about to apologize, though she'd been the one to do it, but even through the blankets, he felt he was in the V of her thighs and all thoughts other than completing his dream fled his brain.

The door opened just as he was bending down to kiss Lexie's sweet lips.

"Oh. I gave you warning," Savs said with a chuckle. "I'm turned around. Get decent. I brought coffee and a bagel since I know Lexie is a beast before she has her first cup."

Lance was trying to process what his sister-in-law was saying, but he couldn't focus, not when he was where he'd wanted to be for so long. Well, almost where he wanted to be. The covers in their way were a huge inconvenience.

"Give us a second," Lexie said with a squeak.

She was yanking at the covers that were trapping her, and trying to push Lance off her. Finally, his brain fired and he moved, grabbed the covers, and then slid beneath, his leg pressed against Lexie's. He didn't need Savvy seeing his morning happiness that was ready to explode with the simplest of touches.

"It's safe to turn around. You just startled us, that's all. Nothing was going on," Lexie said after sending Lance a death glare.

Savvy turned and grinned at both of them. "Sure," she said with sugar. Lance was loving his sister-in-law more and more by the second. He realized she wasn't at all against a relationship between her sister and him. He had at least one cheerleader in his section.

"I'm gonna leave this on the nightstand. We're going to leave in two hours. I've given you plenty of time," Savvy said, winking at them before exiting the room.

Lance turned and looked at how adorably embarrassed Lexie was, and he couldn't help himself. With a quick movement, he shifted and was pressed on top of her, his thickness between her thighs, his lips only inches from hers.

"What are you doing?" she asked, though it was more than obvious.

"Tell me to stop if you don't like it," he said, bending down and kissing her jaw. Damn, she tasted good. He nibbled along her jaw line, his erection pulsing against the heat from her covered core. He tasted his way back up to the corner of her lips before leaning back and looking into her eyes, which were fired up as much as his were.

Pressing himself tightly against her, he wanted to leave no doubt where he was hoping this would lead them. Her eyes sparked again, and they hadn't even kissed yet. He was waiting, wanting to draw out the beautiful moment. If they weren't interrupted again, he might finally get the happy ending they both deserved so damn much. Too bad he hadn't done exactly this the night before.

"Lance . . ." she said with a sigh.

It didn't sound like a protest. Maybe she was giving in to what she wanted as badly as he did but was too afraid to say anything. Lance felt relief wash through him.

"What do you want, Lexie?" he asked, leaning down and gently kissing her lips, just a small taste. Her tongue flicked out and wetted them, and he pulsed against her body.

His hips moved in a circular motion as he pushed against her. Yep. Seduction it was. She was too shy or too something to admit she wanted him, but as he pressed into her, she also wasn't telling him to stop.

He wanted her, but it had to do with so much more than needing her physically. He loved talking with her, laughing with her, watching her expression-filled eyes when she was happy or angry or sad. He was learning so much about her, and the more he learned, the more he wanted her.

But at the moment there was only one thing on his mind. He needed to sate the lust he had for her, and he wanted to make her cry out his name like she'd done a year before. He wanted her thinking of nothing but him, and he wanted to do it over and over. Two hours wasn't remotely long enough.

"Kiss me, Lance." Her words were music to his ears, and he didn't hesitate even a nanometer of a second. His head descended, and she was reaching for him as he closed the distance. Their mouths collided in a passion that had been brewing for too long now that they were finally together in a bed again.

This time they were where they needed to be, and his body was on fire as he pushed against her, feeling the heat of her core. Her breasts were covered with a thin shirt, and he could feel the softness of them cradling his chest. He should take some of his weight off her, but he was losing his mind as her hands wrapped around his back and her nails dug into his hot flesh.

She squirmed beneath him, thrusting her hips up to press against him as she moaned into his mouth. He captured the sound as he swept past her lips and devoured her mouth. His fingers dug into her hair as he pushed his pelvis down. He needed to remove their clothes, and he needed to do it quickly before anything else could interrupt them.

Wrenching his mouth from hers, he loved her whimper of disapproval that quickly changed when he kissed down her jaw and sucked the skin on her neck where her pulse was pounding out of control. He needed her shirt gone, so he lifted up enough to wrench it from her body before he continued trailing his tongue down her collarbone, seeking the beauty of her breasts.

Her nipples were bright pink, and he couldn't resist running his tongue over both of them, seeing them shine as she wiggled beneath him, calling out his name in a low moan. His body pulsed, and he wanted to crawl back up and cradle himself in her thighs but he also needed to taste her again.

"More," she demanded as her hands fisted in his hair, and she held him to her breasts. He gladly obliged, taking one nipple into his mouth and sucking it hard, relishing in her whimpers of pleasure. Her hips bucked up against his chest as she sought sweet relief.

He needed more. Moving down her body he kissed her quivering stomach as he hooked his fingers into her pajama pants. She lifted her hips as he pulled them down and was in awe, gazing at the beauty of her most sensitive place.

Running his finger down her opening, she spread her thighs, giving him full access as she twisted on the bed. Looking up her body, he nearly came in his pants at the sight of her biting her lip as she tried desperately not to cry out.

Sinking a finger inside her, Lance was awed at how wet and hot she was. She would cradle him perfectly when he finally sank deep within her slick folds. He couldn't take it anymore, and he bent his head, running his tongue along her heat, making her entire body jerk off the bed.

"Lance, please . . ." she whimpered as he found her pulsing flesh and sucked on it while two fingers pumped deep inside her. He felt the trembles, knew she was going to come. He wanted to send her over the edge, but this time he wanted to do it while looking into her eyes.

Removing his fingers, he climbed up her body, not taking time to remove his pants. He reached down and slid them out of the way as Lexie wrapped her legs behind his back and gazed at him in a passion induced coma.

"Yes, Lance, now," she told him.

He didn't wait any longer. With a solid thrust, he pushed himself forward and nearly came at the hot entrance into her body. She cried out, this time loudly as her back arched and her naked breasts rubbed against his chest.

Her legs wrapped around him, pushing him all the way inside, and Lance saw stars dance before his eyes.

"It was worth the wait," he growled before he stopped talking and captured her swollen lips. He pushed his tongue in and out of her mouth as he moved his hips faster and faster, pumping inside her tight heat.

She cried out, this time the sound was captured by his mouth as he felt her let go, her body squeezing him rhythmically. Lance lost it, moving his hips quickly as he let go and released deep within her.

Exhausted, he collapsed, their slick skin rubbing against each other as she cradled him tightly between her thighs, her fingers rubbing up and down his back. He twitched inside her as she squeezed him, and he realized he could do it all over again. He'd never get enough of this woman. It would be unending pleasure.

There were voices outside their door, and then a tap on it. Lance was so languid after their lovemaking, he didn't have the energy to cover them. He didn't care. His body was over hers. If his family members were going to be rude enough to open the door, they'd get a nice glimpse of his ass.

"Leaving in one hour," a voice called and then their footsteps faded away down the hall.

With reluctance, Lance pulled back and looked into Lexie's face. She smiled shyly at him.

"I guess the morning session is over," she said with a chuckle. Relief flooded him. She wasn't having instant regrets.

"Don't worry. I can see an afternoon, night, morning, mid-morning—" he began when she cut him off with her laughter.

"Do you plan on breaking me?" she asked.

He leaned down and took her lips in a soft kiss. "Let's break each other," he suggested.

"I might be up for that," she told him.

Lance had an hour. He decided they could each come one more time before they had to face his family. Her eyes lit up when he began pumping inside her again, and the rest of the world faded away.

CHAPTER SIXTEEN

HOT WATER STREAMING over her body, Lexie was more relaxed than she could ever remember. What a perfect way to start the day, she thought, with a hunk of a man sliding in and out of her. And not just any man, but Lance Storm, a sexual god who she couldn't believe she'd been able to resist for so long.

He'd wanted to share the shower with her, but she'd had no doubt that if he did, they would never make it downstairs. As it was, they were going to be late for the deadline his family had set. And she didn't even care about that. It was well worth it. Why had she resisted his lovemaking for so long? Was she truly that big of a fool?

Now that he'd opened up that door, she wanted more. She wanted him to take her in the shower, on the counter, in front of the fireplace, and in that big beautiful bed. She wanted him with an indescribable need. Was she being stupid about it? Yes, she was. She knew that, but it was too late to close that door, so she'd better just suck it up and deal with it.

Or maybe not. If she closed the door on her emotions and her mind, she could simply enjoy this Christmas, which she was certain was going to be the best one of her life, and suffer the consequences later. That was well worth it, she decided. She'd have her cake and eat it too. Then when it was over, she'd have a lot of ice cream as she came down from the high.

That decided, she shut off the shower and stepped out. As she toweled off her body, she pictured Lance's hands all over her. That had her turned on again and wanting to go into that bedroom and attack him. She was sure he wouldn't mind. She wasn't sure what the family had planned, but it couldn't possibly be as fun as the two of them naked together in that big bed. Maybe they could stay there for the entire week. Who needed Santa?

Lexie was slightly relieved when she came out of the bathroom and Lance wasn't there. With the way her thoughts were going, she wasn't sure she'd be able to keep her hands to herself. She'd never thought she'd turn into some sex siren, but now that she'd opened those doors, she didn't want to close them again.

Going downstairs was a bit daunting. She didn't have to try to find anyone because the noise led her in the direction of the dining room where people were grabbing pastries, hot chocolate, and eggnog, and visiting with each other.

She stood in the doorway, making sure to avoid the mistletoe and trying not to feel like an invader. She told herself all those siblings had gotten married and brought new people into the household who had been accepted. But that didn't help because even though she and Lance were having sex, she wasn't his real girlfriend. She was just a way to stop his family from meddling. She didn't want to think about that. It was too damn depressing.

"Ready for more?" Lance whispered in her ear. She hadn't even seen him approach. With those quiet words spoken for only her to hear, her core heated and her breasts tightened.

"Not here," she told him in a fierce whisper. He smiled at her before bending over and giving her a quick kiss. Lexie hated her damn cheeks, because she felt them heat. She'd been expecting this sort of thing. They were supposed to be putting on a show for the family.

The thing was, though, it didn't feel like a show. It felt real, and she could get used to his mouth on hers often and in all sorts of places. No. No. No. She was in the middle of a crowded room and didn't have time for those thoughts.

"What are we in such a hurry to do?" she asked Lance as she took a step back from him.

"That's the miracle of surprises," he told her.

"Is everyone going?" She didn't see how they could all go anywhere without closing down an entire town. How many people were there? It had to be a few dozen. It was too dizzying to try to count.

"We're riding with my brother Crew and his wife, Haley," Lance told her. That wasn't so bad. She'd be with just a few people. Much better than the entire group.

"Nope, there's been a change," Crew said as he stepped up. Lexie had seen Lance's brother Crew but hadn't talked to him before. The man was as good-looking as Lance and had the same sparkling eyes. His wife joined him and gave Lexie a friendly smile.

"Joseph said he hasn't been spending enough time with his *single* nephew," Haley said with a laugh as she emphasized the word and winked at Lance. "He's driving, and we have to pray to survive."

"I'm not single," Lance said in almost a panic as his arm snaked around Lexie. "I have Lexie here."

"There isn't a ring on her finger yet, and you know Uncle Joseph won't be satisfied until that happens," Crew said, obviously enjoying himself.

Lexie found herself rubbing the spot where a wedding ring would sit. She just wasn't sure exactly how she felt about having one there. She'd never wanted to marry, had always looked at it as the most awful thing in the world, growing up with the father she'd been ill-fated to have. But as she gazed at all the happy Anderson couples she couldn't help but wonder if she'd been wrong.

Did one bad example in her life mean she was damned to an eternity alone? Her sister had found one of the good ones. Lexie was sure Lance was also a great guy. But he hadn't wanted marriage any more than she had a month ago. This was getting far too complicated for her to process. She'd rather hide in her room than face those sorts of questions.

"Maybe he won't have to wait much longer," Lance said with a wink sent her way that made her head spin. She told herself this was all part of the act. Still, her throat closed up as she looked at the man who was becoming far too important to her.

Not able to speak, she smiled before turning back to look at Crew and his wife and giving them a wobbly smile.

"Come on, Lance, you're scaring her," Haley scolded as she pulled Lexie away from Lance. Lexie wasn't sure if she was relieved or not by the gesture.

Lance had to be too good to be true. That was the bottom line. Men like him weren't that great. They looked good on paper, but reality was different than fantasy.

"Don't be scared off by these men. They have far too many hormones running rampant," Haley told her. "But take it from me, they are worth getting to know."

Lexie wondered if this woman was a mind reader. She instantly liked Haley. Something about her invited a person to share their deepest and darkest secrets. She'd have to ask her sister who her favorite sister-in-law was.

"This is a bit overwhelming," Lexie admitted and Haley laughed.

"Believe me I know. When I first met Crew, I approached him and asked if he'd teach me how to be a seductress for another man," Haley admitted.

Lexie was floored. "Seriously?" she asked with a gasp.

"Yep. I was all set on winning a man who wasn't worth the prize," Haley told her. "Crew reluctantly agreed, but then I seduced him in the end," she added with a big grin.

"Wow, that sounds like a fairy tale," Lexie said.

"A dirty fairy tale," Haley told her with a laugh.

"What are you girls doing over here?" Joseph asked with a big grin as he joined them.

Lexie was intimidated by the giant man who did a great impression of Santa. All he needed was a red suit and a tobacco pipe, and he'd be good to go at any mall in America.

"We're gossiping about your nephews," Haley told him with a smile.

"Those boys need you ladies to keep them on their toes," Joseph said with a laugh. Then he focused on Lexie. "Are you keeping my Lance on his?"

Lexie's cheeks heated at his intense gaze, and she wasn't sure what to say to this mountain of a man. If he knew what she and his nephew had done that morning he might not be looking at her with such a sweet smile.

"Um . . ." she stuttered, not knowing what to say.

"He needs to do the right thing and let you make an honest man out of him," Joseph said as he pointedly looked at her finger. Lexie was ready to sink into the ground.

"Why don't you quit trying to scare the woman off and maybe I'll do that?" Lance said as he came and saved her for what felt like the millionth time.

"Now that's what I like to hear at the holidays," Joseph told them before patting Lance's shoulder so hard she didn't see how he didn't fall over.

"You'll learn to appreciate Uncle Joseph. He might be a meddler, but he loves us all," Haley said with a sympathetic smile. "Don't run away, just take it all in."

The conversation ended when people started making their way to the front door where vehicles were warmed up and ready to go. Lexie felt a bit of excitement as she watched her sister get into a vehicle with her daughter and husband.

This was a pretty incredible family, but Lexie wasn't sure she fit in with all of them. Her sister had been like a mother to her so it was natural that Savvy fit right in. Lexie had been different. She'd been hidden from so much, but she'd seen a lot more than Savvy would have liked her to have seen. It changed a person in ways she wasn't able to talk about. Maybe someday, but she didn't see it happening anytime soon.

"Ready?" Lance asked.

"Always," she said. Thinking about the word, she realized it was becoming more and more true. She might always be ready for this mysterious man who had shown up in her life and refused to go away. The thing was, now she didn't want him to go anywhere.

CHAPTER SEVENTEEN

L EXIE WAS PACKED into the backseat of the SUV between Lance and Haley while Crew sat in the front chatting with Joseph, who'd turned up the radio station playing non-stop Christmas tunes.

When Rudolph came on in a country twang, Lexie smiled when both Haley and Lance started singing along, purposely messing up the words as the two of them nudged her until she caved and joined in.

She'd never win an award for her musical talent, but she didn't care. There was something about Christmas music that made a person get into the spirit of the holidays. And with Lance's deep, surprisingly good voice sounding in her ear she couldn't seem to stop smiling.

As he reached over and rested his hand on her thigh, the touch scorching her, she squirmed in the seat. She needed to push his hand away, but Haley was looking at the two of them with a secret smile that had Lexie panicking. She couldn't give away their deception in front of his sister-in-law and his uncle, who she was sure had eyes in the back of his head.

"We might need to sing some karaoke soon, or start our own band," Joseph said in a voice that had Lexie jumping where she sat. The man was louder than anyone she'd heard before. He certainly would never need a microphone.

"I think I'll stick to the bathroom shower," Lexie said without thinking. Lance turned and gave her a sizzling look that made her cheeks glow.

"I'll do a duet with you then," he told her with a wink. She was too mortified to turn and see what Haley thought about that comment.

"Haley and I perform those kind of duets every chance we get," Crew said from the front seat, laughing with joy.

Lexie was shocked at how they could say such things in front of their uncle. But Joseph just continued singing the next song, acting as if he hadn't heard a word. Lexie wasn't used to sharing such intimate thoughts, or saying whatever came to mind. It was a good thing she wouldn't be around this family too long because she was sure she couldn't get used to that.

"We're not far away now," Joseph told them.

Good, Lexie thought. She wasn't necessarily uncomfortable, it was just that she was having to work harder to keep her guard up the longer she was with these people. Locked in a vehicle while Joseph quizzed her, and Lance's brother made every innuendo known to man, was taking the last of her self-control away.

They arrived in a giant parking lot and Joseph turned off the car. He and Crew got out and opened the back doors before Lance or Haley could reach for the knobs. When Lexie stepped out, Lance took her hand, and she looked around. There were lights up ahead but she wasn't sure where they were.

"What is going on?" she asked. No one had filled her in on what they were doing.

"It's another family tradition that normally winds up with some sore behinds, but the spiked eggnog almost makes it worth it," Lance said.

She dug her heels in. "I'm not moving until you tell me," she said.

Joseph laughed as he looked at the two of them, and she was a bit embarrassed to be throwing a small tantrum in front of his family. But Lexie wasn't keen on surprises, especially ones that could end with her injured.

"Don't worry, if you get sore, I'll be sure to rub it out for you," he said for her ears only.

And just like that, Lexie's worry faded as heat invaded her. The snow gently falling around them could have been a tropical shower because she would have sworn steam was rising from her flushed skin. With only words and a light touch, Lance could make her go up in flames. The man had too much power over her. She didn't appreciate that fact.

"You won't be touching anything," she whispered back.

"You sure wanted me to earlier," he reminded her.

Lexie looked around to make sure their conversation wasn't overheard. Lance wasn't holding back any punches, and it was slightly mortifying as it was his family she was with. She almost wished she had her own clan to drag him to so she could put him through the same embarrassment. Then again, she had a feeling he wouldn't mind. No matter where they were, she was sure Lance would fit right in. He was just that sort of guy.

"Please," she said, hating that she was begging.

He gave her a smile. "It's a small community that gets into the holidays. They have booths and food, drinks and singing . . . and ice-skating," he told her as he tugged on her hand, making her move forward.

Lexie obediently followed as Joseph plowed his way through the snow so he could meet with the rest of the family. She had a bad feeling the afternoon wasn't going to be as pleasant as Joseph was hoping.

While she wasn't the klutziest person on earth, she never had mastered the art of skating, and with his entire family probably able to do triple axels, she was going to feel like the odd man out. Her only saving grace was she knew her sister hadn't learned either. But Savvy most likely had been there last year and had some practice beneath her belt. Lexie had zip, zero, zilch.

"I think I'd much rather sit in the cheering section and applaud you," she said, stooping to batting her eyelashes as she attempted a pathetic version of flirtation.

"Don't worry; if you start to fall, I'll catch you," he tried to assure her.

Lexie let it go. She didn't want to be one of those people who complained too much just because she didn't necessarily like what was happening. If she fell, so be it. Hopefully there would be others who would be down with her.

All the family was at the entrance to the place when they got there, and the kids were giddy with joy. Lexie noticed when the oldest grandchild, Jasmine, snuck off to flirt with one of the boys wearing a Santa hat serving hot chocolate. That didn't last long, though, because her father, Lucas, spotted what was going on and marched over, sending the boy a terrifyingly dark look. The boy couldn't have been more than seventeen and quickly thanked Jasmine for her order, then refused to look her in the eyes again.

Lexie looked over to see Joseph chuckling with his two brothers as the scene unfolded. Then the old man whispered something that had his two brothers looking at their grandchild/niece.

As Lexie and Lance passed them, she heard Joseph's words, and wondered if Lance had been right about the old men being meddlers. He told his brothers it wouldn't be long before the next generation would be ready to settle down and give them more babies.

Lexie decided it might be a lot safer to stay off those men's radar. They had one son/nephew left in their family who was single, and she was there with that particular man. She couldn't think that way because then she might start believing in Christmas miracles and hoping for a future that wasn't in the cards for her.

Lexie procrastinated as long as possible before Lance dragged her over to the huge outdoor ice rink, filled with his family and many other happy Christmas folks. Before she knew it, she was holding skates in her hand and being led to a bench.

Her stomach clenched as she took her time putting them on, lacing them up, and then gazing at Lance's hand as if it were a snake. She was going to fall down. She had no doubt about it. At least she had a nice massage to look forward to when it happened.

"You will be fine," Lance assured her.

"I'm just warning you now that if I fall, I'm taking you down with me," she threatened. If he was so keen on holding her hand, he'd been warned.

Lexie was wobbly as the two of them made their way onto the ice. Her sister flew by, laughing as Ashton pulled her into his arms and skated backward, perfectly she might add, just so he could kiss her.

Lexie smiled at the pure joy on Savvy's face as she looked at the husband she loved so much. Lexie felt a stab of jealousy that her sister had everything she'd never known she'd wanted. It was beautiful and special, and Lexie wondered if she would ever come close to feeling that much joy.

As she had the thought, her gaze was captured by Lance. He let go of her hand, which sent her into a panic, before his arms came around her and hugged her close.

Just like that her nerves evaporated and she was lost in his eyes. He was so beautiful, showed so much affection in his eyes, and made her feel like she was the only woman on the planet when he looked at her. She forgot to protect her heart when she was lost in his gaze.

"You are stunning," he said, leaning down and kissing her. Lexie didn't hesitate to kiss him back. When he pulled away, she felt as if she were in a dream.

"Did you find more mistletoe?" his cousin Drew asked as he skated by.

Lexie turned and smiled at him. "We're looking for it."

That made both him and Lance laugh, and Lexie tightened that seal on her coffin a little more. She was growing too comfortable if she was able to think so quickly without being embarrassed.

Lance pulled away with what felt like reluctance and took her hand again as they slowly moved around the rink. They circled a couple times before Lexie began to feel confident on the ice. She began looking up, noticing all the people doing twirls and spins in the center, and she realized she was having a great time.

"Ready to play?" Lance asked.

"Maybe," she told him. "Why don't you show me what you can do?"

The look Lance gave her should have frightened her, but even though Lexie was completely out of her element, she was also with Lance, and as long as he was holding on to her she felt invincible.

Lance let her go and skated forward. He'd been holding back. He did some twists and turns and Lexie laughed as he met up with his brothers, and they began a game of hot potato. Lexie got a bit braver and joined them, although going much slower than everyone else.

The ball was suddenly tossed to her and surprisingly she caught it. Before she was able to pass it off, she felt her feet begin to slide out from beneath her. Here came the sore bottom she'd been afraid of. But more than that, she worried her hands would be on the ice and someone skating by would hit them.

All of these thoughts flashed through her mind as she windmilled, trying to stop the inevitable fall. She was almost on the ice when Lance flew in from nowhere and grabbed her. The momentum was too great to stop the fall, but he twisted at the last second and was the one to land hard on the ice. She went down on top of him, but not gracefully.

Lance made a noise from deep inside his gut unlike anything she'd ever heard before as her knee connected with his groin. His brothers were heading in their direction, and as Lexie looked up she saw the wince on each of their faces as they cringed in sympathy for their brother.

"I'm so sorry, so very, very sorry," Lexie told Lance as she tried to get off him. She only made it worse though, when she slipped and went down again, hitting him this time in the eye with her elbow.

Much to the man's credit, he didn't toss her off him, just reached up and grabbed her shoulders as he looked at her with pain in his eyes.

"Please," he groaned, his voice barely recognizable, "stop helping me."

Lexie froze as she forced her body to relax. She looked into his eyes and wondered if this was it, if he was finally going to figure out what an utter mess she really was. Arms reached beneath hers, and she was lifted off Lance as Alex, another cousin, skated to a perfect stop in front of them and reached down to assist Lance.

"Damn, cuz, that didn't look like it felt too good," Alex said, though there was obvious mirth in his voice.

"You think?" Lance snapped as he accepted his cousin's hand. His voice was already beginning to return to normal.

"I'm so sorry," Lexie said again, horrified that she'd maimed him. "I told you I shouldn't get on the ice. I'm so sorry." She had warned him, but that didn't mean she should prevent him from having children because he'd wanted her to try a new activity.

"Don't worry about it, Sis, I think he'll survive," her sister said as she joined the crowd. His entire family was there, seeing what she'd done. Lexie was utterly horrified and wanted nothing more than to go home.

"I think I'm done skating for the day," Lance said, then shocked Lexie when he grinned at her. "Unless there're any other parts of my body you want to damage," he added with a wink.

"So sorry," she muttered again.

Most of his family had been trying to hold in their laughter but they finally let loose, and soon half of them were bent over as they chortled so loudly the rest of the rink of skaters were turning to look in their direction.

"We'd better go find some snow for Lance to sit in for a while," Joseph said, even his voice filled with mirth.

"I think I'll pass," Lance said with a roll of his eyes. "But I think I might be the one in need of that massage," he added as he looked at Lexie.

The entire family turned and looked at her, and she was grateful for the cold, because her heated cheeks could be blamed on the low temperatures and not her mortification.

Lance easily moved over to her and wrapped his arm around her before leaning in and giving her a light peck on the lips. "Best time I've ever had here," he said to her.

Now that the drama was over, the rest of the family drifted off, some to get a few more twirls in on the ice, but most to go and change out of their skates so they could get a hot drink before they drove home.

"I think you might have hit your head," Lexie told Lance as they sat down, and she quickly began unlacing the weapons on her feet.

"I kept you from getting hurt," he said proudly.

"At your own expense," she reminded him.

"Ah, you can't hurt me," he told her. He was back to normal within minutes. It was insane. But as she looked at his beautiful face, she noticed purple beginning to show around his eye and she reached up and gently ran her thumb across it.

"I really am sorry," she told him again.

"Why don't you just kiss my injuries to make them all better?" he said with a waggle of his brows.

Lexie finally relaxed as she smiled at him.

"You are insufferable," she told him.

"I try," he told her before a wicked gleam appeared in his eyes. "You might have to nurse me back to health."

"Oh really?" she asked. "And what exactly do you need?"

He reached for her, tugging her easily onto his lap before kissing her hard, but far too quickly. She was still breathless.

"First of all, I think I'm gonna have to get you a naughty nurse outfit so you can act the part."

Lexie laughed before she kissed him. Leaning back, she gazed at this man who made her feel so many new emotions.

"I think you faked being hurt," she told him.

"No, I'm in pain. I need my nurse," he said as he crossed his fingers over his heart.

"Well then, first order is to get you home and ice the merchandise," she said as she reluctantly pulled herself from his lap. She noticed the lump in his pants. "Obviously you're not *that* injured."

"I can't control my body. You sit on my lap, and my lower half gets ideas," he said with a chuckle. "It also doesn't help that I'm now picturing you in a nurse outfit that doesn't leave anything to the imagination."

Lexie hadn't ever been into role-play, but for this man, she might be willing to do just about anything. She pushed the fear away as he stood up, and they walked side by side from the rink. She was too content to dwell on her worries — at least for now.

CHAPTER EIGHTEEN

NEVER IN HIS life had Lance thought it would be a blessing to get kneed in the groin. But he found himself grateful it had happened, because they were back at the lodge with his family, the kids all curled up on beanbag chairs on the floor, the adults sitting on various furniture, but most importantly, Lexie was curled up at his side, rubbing his thigh as they laughed through the Christmas movie, *Arthur Christmas.*

He'd never watched it before, but it was quickly turning into his favorite of all time as Lexie laughed and grew misty-eyed beside him on the couch. He was fully conscious of her hand on his thigh, though the best part was she was doing it unconsciously. She wasn't worried about putting on a show, or even thinking about what anyone else thought of them.

They were surrounded by family, but he felt as if it were just the two of them in their own little bubble. Lance had gone a long time thinking he didn't need anyone around him, but now he enjoyed his family, and he *really* enjoyed the woman at his side.

It was a delicate matter, he decided, because he didn't want to scare her away, but he also didn't want her to think she wasn't important. If he had his way, he'd be dropping to his knees in front of her right now and demanding she stay with him forever.

The most shocking part was how right that felt. Just a few short months, hell, weeks ago, he'd been against marriage, against doing what his family deemed his responsibility to settle down. Now, he couldn't think of anything other than marriage and babies.

Lance ran his fingers through Lexie's soft hair and felt warmth spread inside him as she sighed and snuggled closer. He was so relaxed, there could be a tornado ripping through the living room and he didn't think he'd care enough to move.

Lance finally understood what his siblings had been talking about since they'd met the person they couldn't live without. What had once felt like shackles now felt freeing. Maybe later he'd have to kick himself, but for now, he knew his life wouldn't be complete if he screwed things up and let this woman go.

The movie ended and his cousins and siblings began rounding up their kids to get them ready for bed. A couple years ago, he'd been thankful he hadn't been a part of the masses looking frazzled as family members tried to get the kids to bed so they could have a few moments alone. Now, it was the opposite. He wished he had a little girl with Lexie's eyes who would cuddle against his shoulder as he carried her off to a princess bed and tucked her in.

He wanted to be the one reading a bedtime story and hearing her say she loved him. He wanted things that had seemed worse than death at one time. But he now realized there was no purpose to life if he planned on living alone forever. A lonely existence he wanted no part of.

Soon the room cleared and Lance was alone with Lexie, who seemed content to do nothing more than stay right where she was. He wanted to pick her up, carry her to their room, and make sweet love to her.

"I think I need that medical attention now," he whispered as his fingers ran down her shoulder and drifted across the top of her luscious breasts. This wasn't the place to get worked up.

People could walk in at any time, but he couldn't seem to help himself.

"Oh really?" she asked in a relaxed voice.

"Yeah, I'm really hurting here . . . I think I'm swollen," he told her, trying to sound pathetic but unable to keep the smile out of his voice.

"That's terrible," she told him with a chuckle. "I wouldn't want anything to have to be cut off."

Lance winced at that thought. "No, we definitely don't want *that* to happen," he said emphatically.

Lexie pulled away from him, and he didn't want to let her go, but then she stood up and held out a hand to him, and he knew right then if he'd been in the Garden of Eden, he would have accepted the apple without a twinge of guilt. He'd follow this woman anywhere she wanted to lead him.

The two of them strolled through the large lodge, and though Lance was throbbing and wanted to sink inside her more than he wanted to take his next breath, he found himself also enjoying the walk to their shared room together. He wasn't in a hurry. He enjoyed the anticipation. He was definitely going to have to turn in his man card at this rate.

That thought made him smile. As long as he kept his ridiculous thoughts to himself, he was fine. His brothers and cousins would rag him to no end, even though they were just as infatuated with their women as he was with Lexie.

They reached their room and Lance shut the door behind them. Lexie gave him a sexy glance before she disappeared into the bathroom. He wanted to strip off his clothes and stand in front of the fire, but he also didn't know what was on her mind, so he decided to wait.

Dang, he was having fun with this woman. He loved the uncertainty of it all, and that surprised him. Normally, he thrived on being in control at all times and in all ways. But with Lexie, part of the appeal was in knowing she wasn't going to do whatever pleased him to get his attention. She was her own person, and if she was with him it was because she wanted and needed to be.

Lexie stepped out of the bathroom in nothing but one of his white, button-down shirts, halfway undone, with a red medical cross drawn on the pocket; he nearly embarrassed himself and exploded in his pants.

Her hair was in a sloppy bun, and she was holding a note-pad and pen in her hand. He began to move toward her, and she shook her head, making him stop instantly. He was a willing puppet drooling at her feet.

"I hear you have an injury to your . . ." She paused as her eyes drifted down his body and focused on the part of him that was throbbing.

"Yes, yes, I do," he gasped.

"Hmm. I better check and make sure everything is in working order, Mr. Storm," she said with a mischievous smile. Hot damn, he was definitely going to marry this woman!

Trying desperately not to rush over and attack her, Lance forced himself not to move as she sidled over to him. Leaning her head back, she lifted one hand and rubbed it down the open V of his shirt, which had never looked so damn sexy as it did resting against her glorious breasts.

"It's a bit warm in here, don't you think?" she asked as she took a few steps closer to him.

"Hell yes, it is," he exclaimed, more than ready to rip off his clothes. He was already sweating, but it had nothing to do with the temperature of the room. It was all due to the magnificent, beautiful woman who was enjoying their game of doctor.

"Hmm," she murmured as she trailed a finger down his chest and brushed over the thickness throbbing in his pants, before pulling back and lifting her pen to jot something down on her notepad. "I'm detecting a fever."

"Yeah, I definitely have a fever," he said on a groan.

She circled him, and he craned his neck to follow, but she pushed his face forward so he couldn't see her. Then she pressed her glorious body against his back and reached around him, her hand cupping his erection which was about to rip the seams of his pants.

"This definitely feels swollen," she said, her hot breath rushing across his neck.

"Yes, and in pain," he said through clenched teeth.

"We'll have to see what we can do about that," she told him.

She let him go, and he wanted to let out a cry of disapproval but then she pushed against his back, and he obediently moved forward. She led him to the large chair in the corner of the room and turned him around before pushing him so he landed on his butt, his feet outstretched.

"Let me get a closer look," she said. She dropped down to her knees and leaned forward, giving him a glorious view of her full breasts before the material of the shirt covered them again. He was seconds away from reaching forward and shredding the material.

As if reading his mind, she looked up and licked her lips, smiling at him. "Good patients get rewards. Bad ones don't get help," she told him with a tsk.

Her fingers reached into the waistband of his pants, and she told him to scooch up. He pushed off the floor and she tugged, bringing his pants and underwear down, making his erection spring free.

Lance was mesmerized as she knelt between his thighs, her painted lips open in an appreciative gasp as she stuck out her tongue and licked them while reaching out and taking his thickness in her hand. He dribbled some of his excitement and she smiled, never breaking eye contact as she leaned over and ran her tongue in a circle around his pulsing erection.

Lance couldn't look away as she laid gentle kisses on the tip before moving down the length of him, her tongue coming out and forging the path for her. He moaned in tortured happiness.

"I think I see the problem," she purred.

Lance couldn't process her words, couldn't figure out what she was trying to say. He was too lost in the pleasure of what she was doing as her hand moved slowly up and down his shaft while she continued licking the tip.

"We've got to get this swelling to go down," she continued before she closed her lips and sucked, making a sound in her throat that rumbled through him. She didn't stay there long, preferring to torture him as her mouth popped off and her hand continued rubbing along his length.

"Please, Lexie . . ." he begged. He reached down and cupped her head in his hands as he tugged her to him. He needed her mouth.

She smiled at him one more time before opening those beautiful lips and taking him in, his tip reaching her throat where it tightened around him. She bobbed her head, moving steadily up and down his shaft while one hand squeezed him and the other moved to his stomach so she could run her fingernails across his shaking skin.

He leaned his head back for a minute, emitting a guttural sound before he had to look at her again. She took him deep before looking up, meeting his gaze. The passion in her eyes nearly had him coming.

Pulling away with her mouth, she continued stroking his length as she kissed his tip and then groaned. "You taste so incredible," she purred.

"I'm gonna come before we get to the good part," he said, trying to talk his body out of doing just that. She winked at him.

"This isn't the good stuff?" she questioned with a twinkle in her eyes.

"Oh, baby, it's all good," he quickly assured her. "But I need to be buried inside you."

"Mmm, how about both?" she suggested before closing her mouth over him again.

Lance felt that stirring deep inside him and knew he wasn't going to last if she didn't stop quickly. He wanted to let go, wanted her to take every drop from him, but he also wanted to taste her before he ripped that shirt away and buried himself deep.

Lance decided he was in her hands, and he quit fighting the build-up. Her head moved faster as she took turns bobbing up and down on him, then sucking his head and licking her way from root to tip. Her hands were slippery as she alternated between her mouth and fingers.

He got lost in the fantasy of it all as his hands fisted in her hair, holding her close to his body. He groaned as his stomach began shaking. She popped off him, and he was about to pull her up and thrust inside her.

"Come in my mouth," she demanded before taking him deep.

Letting out a roar of pleasure, his body took over. The first spurt of pleasure shot from him, his thickness pulsing in her mouth as she moaned around him. She circled her tongue around his head, and he pulsed over and over again.

She took it all as he unleashed on her, his fingers tugging her hair, his body hard and unrelenting. She slowed her movements before releasing him, running her tongue up and down his length again in languid movements.

After a few breathtaking moments she continued holding him as she looked up and smiled. His heart thumped, waiting to hear what she would say next.

"Hmm, it appears that didn't alleviate the problem," she said, lifting a finger to her lip and sucking the tip, making him pulse in her hand. "Looks like I'll have to try something else."

"Hell yes!" he told her. He tried to grab her but she scooted back, then stood, rubbing her hand against her thigh, lifting the edge of his shirt up to the sweet spot before letting it fall again.

He was done with the teasing.

Lance jumped up and stalked her as she walked backward toward the bed, her eyes on fire, her nipples peaked and poking against the white material. He reached her as her legs bumped into the bed, and he grabbed her arms, not hesitating before he leaned down and kissed her with uncontrollable passion.

She shook against him as she raised her arms and circled them behind his head. But her turn to be in control was over. It was his show now.

He reached behind him and unclasped her fingers before pushing her backward. Startled, she let out a cry as she fell onto the bed. Lance was right there, and he crawled over her, sitting on her thighs.

"I love the uniform, but it's got to go," he told her. Her legs were trapped and before she could do a thing, he grabbed the folds of the shirt and pulled. It ripped down the center, the buttons flying across the room.

Her eyes heated even more. She reached for him again, but Lance tsked at her. "My turn, remember?" he said with a wicked smile.

He tugged the shirt off her, then grabbed her hands and used the shredded material to tie them above her head. She looked at him in shock.

"What are you doing?" she asked.

"Anything I want," he said with a purr before he secured her arms to the bed and then dropped down, finally able to worship her breasts.

She didn't argue anymore as he molded her breasts and nipples with his fingers, mouth, and teeth. She was writhing in pleasure beneath him as he ran his tongue down her smooth stomach until he reached her hot center.

He didn't stop until he made her come twice, not even when she begged for mercy. Only then did he climb back up her body and look into her glorious eyes as he sank inside her. Home. He was home.

Lance gripped her sweet hip and pulled her to him as he thrust in and out of her body, knowing it would never be enough. They both lost all meaning of time as the night faded into the morning, and he loved her over and over again.

He would never let her go — whether she was willing or not.

CHAPTER NINETEEN

"IT SURE IS nice to have you back home and so happy," Richard said to his son as the two of them stood in the heated barn. Richard was supervising as Lance chopped firewood. Though the lodge had gas fireplaces in practically every bedroom, Joseph insisted on a real fireplace for the living room, and he wanted it going practically twenty-four/seven. He said it brought ambiance.

Lance figured that was because his uncle wasn't the one slaving away chopping wood to keep the dang thing burning. All the kids had to do that chore. Of course, Lance was in such a good mood this trip, he actually didn't mind that much. He wasn't going to tell anyone that though, or he'd be chopping every day instead of his siblings and cousins taking their rightful turns.

"This isn't such a bad holiday, and Uncle Joseph is even merrier than usual," Lance said with a chuckle.

"It might have to do with the fact that you brought home a woman for the first time, and not just any woman, but one that fits right in with the family," Richard said knowingly.

"Don't get started on that, Dad," Lance said with a laugh. Though Lance had already decided he was going to marry the woman, he liked making his family suffer a bit. His father and uncles deserved it. All the kids had figured out long ago they were meddling old men. Payback someday was gonna be a lot of fun for them, they'd determined.

"Are you putting on the wedding pressure?" Crew asked as he and Ashton stepped into the barn, walked up beside their dad, and leaned against the wall.

"I wouldn't dream of that," Richard said innocently.

"Ha," all three boys said in a chorus.

"We're not as blind as you think we are, Dad," Ashton informed the man.

"But since the heat is directed at Lance we don't mind so much," Crew added.

"You guys could actually help me cut wood instead of plotting with our father," Lance grumbled.

"We don't want to take the pleasure away from you. You're doing a fine job," Ashton said, not looking like he was going to budge anytime soon.

"I'll remember that when you're the one out here," Lance threatened.

"We're only here a few more days. I won't have another turn," Ashton said with a smirk.

"Ass," Lance told him.

"Aren't you two just adorable when you bicker?" Crew said with a laugh.

"Shove it," Ashton and Lance said together. They really did think on the same wavelength.

"I have to say, though," Crew said as he looked at Lance, "you and Lexie seem pretty serious. When we heard you were bringing a woman here for the holidays I thought it would be a hooker you hired since a nice girl wouldn't put up with your ass for any length of time. But I like this one. Don't let her get away."

Lance dropped the axe and looked at his brother in surprise. Crew didn't often get serious, especially about women, but even though he wouldn't admit it out loud, he liked that his family cared about Lexie. He wanted them to love the woman he married. That was another change in his life — valuing the opinion of those he'd grown up with. He didn't want to delve into how much he'd changed over the past few years.

"A hooker cost too much," Lance said with a smile. Though he wouldn't mind fleshing out his thoughts, there was no way he was going to in front of his dad. That would give the old man justification in his meddling ways.

"Just remember this is Savvy's sister, so if you don't have honorable intentions, things could get messy quickly," Crew told him.

"I know that," Lance said, getting a little irritated.

"Sometimes it helps to be reminded," Ashton piped in.

"Are you playing the protective older brother?" Lance asked with a laugh.

"I care about her," Ashton admitted. "And I love *and* fear my wife. If you mess with her sister, she's going to come after us both."

"That's a good point," Richard said. Lance had almost forgotten about his father's presence as he conversed with his brothers.

"Look," Lance said as he gave all three men a good stare, "I like Lexie and have no intention of hurting her. Just because you guys are all settled and shit, doesn't mean I need to get the third degree from you."

"I used to be an ass," Crew said, surprising Lance. "As we all did. I met Haley and that all changed. But sometimes when I think about the way I treated women, I'm surprised I survived so long. Now that I'm a dad, I'm really mortified by my past behavior."

"Considering I'm older and wiser than you, you should be taking my advice instead of the other way around," Lance said.

"Ha," Richard broke in as he laughed. "None of you ever listened worth beans, so that's funny you're trying to pull the older brother card."

"We might have had our moments, but in the end we've always respected you, Dad," Crew said.

Richard's brows came together as he looked at three of his sons. They all shifted on their feet before Richard continued.

"I love you and I'm proud of you, but you could all accept advice a bit more graciously," he lectured.

"Yeah, maybe," Crew admitted.

"It took a while to figure out that the right woman was better than a *lot* of women," Ashton said with a laugh. "I thought I'd be losing out by settling down, but damn, I'm away from Savvy for a couple hours and I need to find her again."

"That's 'cause you're whipped," Lance said with a laugh. There was no way he was going to admit he already missed Lexie. She was shopping with her sister, and he had been listening for their car for the past couple hours.

Crew and Ashton looked at him like they could read his thoughts. Dammit. This sibling stuff could really grate on the nerves sometimes.

"Are you going to ask her to marry you?" Richard asked point-blank.

Lance didn't want to lie. He did plan on asking her to be his wife. He just didn't know when — he also wasn't sure of her answer. The two of them were having fun, and the sex was phenomenal, but she was skittish on commitment, more than he had been. He decided to give a partial truth.

"The scary thing about relationships is that all we see are roses and diamonds in the beginning. That's when we're happiest, before any real problems set in. Then boom!" he said, raising his voice. "The roof collapses and you wonder how you ended up with this stranger you don't really know or like."

"Are you telling us you're psychic and can predict the future?" Crew asked with a laugh.

"Just saying what I've seen time and time again," Lance said.

"That happens when you settle. But when you have the right one, nothing is insurmountable," Ashton pointed out.

"Maybe," Lance said. He might have to do a follow-up conversation when his father wasn't there smirking with that all-too-knowing grin on his face.

"Why in the hell can't you just fess up? We see the way you act around this woman. We know you've been tamed," Crew said with a laugh.

He used the excuse that he didn't want to make his dad giddy by admitting how he truly felt about Lexie, but he wondered if that was all it was.

Was there a small part of him that feared what he'd been thinking was actually true? Did he think this relationship would stand the test of time? Or was he waiting to see if he would do something to screw it up and then tell himself he'd gotten away free and clear? Lance wasn't sure what to think. He just knew he was uncomfortable with his brothers' and father's knowing gazes pointed his way.

"I can admit there's something different about her, and that I . . . I like being with her," Lance finally said.

The barn was uncomfortably quiet for several heartbeats after he opened his big mouth. He waited for the ribbing to begin, but his brothers looked serious as they gazed at him like he was already stepping up to the altar.

"I'm not a lost cause," he said, unable to stand the silence any longer.

Ashton smiled. "That's to be determined," he said. "I will give you this advice though," he continued. "If you wait too long, that girl will slip through your fingers and you'll wonder what in the hell happened. Trust me, I almost lost my woman. I can't imagine my life without her."

"Ditto," Crew said.

Their father stood there without having to say anything, but Lance was sure his old man was giving himself a silent pat on the back. His boys had grown up, even if they had done it while kicking and screaming like toddlers.

"Either help me finish this or get out," Lance said, but it was done with a smile.

And he also breathed a sigh of relief when they left him alone. He had wood to chop and had to keep his ears open for Lexie's return. It had only been a few hours and he missed her. Yeah, he was in trouble — and he didn't care.

CHAPTER TWENTY

L EXIE STOOD IN the backyard, the sky bright with the moon behind the clouds, snow falling from the heavens and making the temperature outside almost unbearable. But she wasn't ready to go into the house yet.

She was worried — very worried. She'd spent the day shopping with her sister and some of the other women in the house, and she'd thought about Lance non-stop. Of course the ladies had quizzed her, but she'd sidetracked them by asking about their kids.

Her sister had given her a suspicious glance but she'd let it go. All day, Lexie's thoughts had returned to Lance. She was growing to depend on him, to miss him, to want to be with him entirely too much. She wasn't sure how she felt about that, but it would be accurate to say panic was seeping in.

Since she couldn't control where her thoughts were leading her, she'd managed to avoid Lance since she'd been back, even if it meant shivering in the backyard of the giant lodge while delicate flakes of snow drifted down on her.

"Having a nice time?"

Startled, Lexie nearly face-planted as she whipped around and found Lance leaning on the porch rail as he gazed at her. How long had he been there watching her? Had she been so lost in her thoughts that she was easy to sneak up on?

"The house was a little warm so I needed to cool off," she told him.

He looked at her in disbelief. She wasn't sure how she would respond if he called her on it. She was feeling restless and the urge to run was great. But was that because she was flawed or because there was an actual reason to run? If she knew that answer, her problem would be solved.

"Everyone is doing their own thing tonight so you have plenty of time to . . . cool off," he said, hesitating just enough that she knew he knew she was avoiding him.

"I was supposed to help make cookies tonight so I shouldn't be out here too long," she pointed out.

"That's been put off until tomorrow. Lucas forgot the sugar from the store, and it's a key ingredient," he told her. There went her excuse to avoid going up to the room. The minute Lance touched her she would melt, and none of her confusion would go away.

"Oh, I guess I'll relax and watch a movie with the kiddos again," she said, feeling inspired.

"I don't mind cuddling up on the couch," he told her. Heat filled her, bringing truth to her statement about needing to cool off. She suddenly wanted to tug off her coat and gloves.

"That sounds nice, but I have a bit of a headache. Maybe I should take something and sit in the library for a while."

He grinned and stepped away from the porch, moving toward her. In a panic she whirled around, creating a whirlwind of snow to avoid his touch. She was too confused at the moment.

"You wouldn't be trying to avoid me, would you?" he asked casually, but he didn't reach for her.

"Not at all," she told him. He moved a step closer and she panicked.

Stooping down, she gathered up some snow and quickly packed it in a ball. His eyes narrowed as he saw what she was doing. The man was smart enough to take a couple of retreating steps.

"What are you doing?" he asked, keeping his eyes focused on her.

"Nothing," she said, her worries evaporating as she looked at him with new delight. She hadn't had a snowball fight in a long time. She had no doubt he could pummel her, but if she launched one fast enough, surprising him, she could get away.

"I always win when I play," he warned her.

That made Lexie's eyes narrow. "Too much confidence is a downfall," she warned back.

"Not when it's true," he told her.

That was it. This man deserved a good pummeling. Before her brain could fully process the thought, Lexie's arm lifted and the ball went flying through the air, smacking him right in his cocky mouth. She laughed in delight as he gazed at her, too stunned to speak. Her stomach lurched, but her merriment came out loudly.

"I thought you *always* won," she taunted as she gathered more snow and launched another ball, this one hitting him on the neck, snow trickling down the opening in his coat, making him squeal, which caused her to laugh harder.

"Oh, my darling Lexie, now you've awoken the beast," he warned.

The gleam in his eyes was her only warning as he took a menacing step toward her. Lexie knew retreat was her only option. She should have run while he was still in shock, but the man was surprisingly fast at shaking things off.

With a quick left dodge, she decided there was no way she was getting to the back door. She'd have to go through him to do it. Her only option was to run along the path to the front of the house. The guys had put out that no-slip stuff, so she might make it if she concentrated.

"I love a good chase," he called out after her, his voice far closer than she would have guessed.

Picking up speed, she let go of caution and decided she had to get away. Otherwise this would be a game he *would* certainly win — but would she be the loser if she was in his arms again? Nope. Couldn't think thoughts like that right now. It was war and she was winning.

Lexie only made it a few more feet before she felt his hot breath on her neck and his arms clasping around her. Laughter spilled from her as her feet were pulled from the ground, her back pressed against the solid muscle of Lance's chest. She could practically feel his body heat pouring through their winter clothes.

"Now what should I do for an easy victory?" he whispered in her ear, his hot breath a contrast to the cold snow still falling on them.

"You haven't won. You're the one with snow down your shirt," she told him as she struggled to get free.

Lance chuckled as he walked toward the soft snow on the side of the path.

"I guess I'll have to remedy that," he told her.

Lexie had no time to figure out what he was talking about before the two of them fell as he launched them into the soft snow. Her face was covered as snow crept into her clothes, sending shivers through her body.

Lexie pushed against Lance, who was just as covered as she was, calling it a tie in her book, but then she was on top of him, throwing more snow in his face as she laughed.

Lance's shock completed her victory, but he grabbed her back and tugged her forward, laying her body on his as the two of them sank deeper into the snow, nearly disappearing from sight.

"Now I need warming up," he told her before his hand reached into her hair and tugged her the last couple inches forward.

His lips claimed hers and she soon forgot all about the snow coating them as he heated her entire body with a swipe of his tongue and the skill of his lips. He didn't have to command anything, because the moment he touched her, she belonged to him:

heart, body, and soul. She was exactly where she wanted to be, even if she'd been foolish enough to fight it.

His thickness pressed between her thighs as she straddled him while he ravaged her mouth. More. She didn't want to think anymore. She just wanted to feel — to feel the happiness of playing in the snow with him, to feel the security of having his arms around her, and to feel the passion only his touch could bring.

Just as she was reaching for his coat to undo it, he broke their kiss. She tried to reconnect, but he held her face between his hands. There was fire burning in his eyes; she didn't understand how the snow wasn't melted all around them.

"We need to go inside to finish this," he said.

She struggled to process what he said. "No. I don't want to stop," she said, pushing back to him. For a moment they were lost in the kiss, then she was moving upward as he gripped her and sat up.

Somehow he was able to get on his feet with her still in his arms, and their lips reconnected as he walked toward the house without stopping. Lexie had no idea if anyone saw them come in or go up the stairs. She'd tried to fight what she felt for Lance and had failed miserably. By the time he finished warming her up she had forgotten what she'd been worried about in the first place. She fell asleep tucked securely in his arms.

CHAPTER TWENTY-ONE

I T WAS THREE days until Christmas, and the closer it came the less holiday spirit Lexie felt. She knew she was acting like Scrooge, at least in her thoughts, but no matter how hard she tried to tamp the impending doom, she couldn't stop it. It seemed the more she tried to prepare herself for the holiday ending, the less Lance allowed her to pull away.

Her entire body was shaking as the two of them stepped inside after taking the kids on a walk to gather pinecones for ornament-making later that evening. It had been so much fun to be outdoors, to have his hand in hers, and to watch the kids attack the men with snowballs as the ladies helped from behind the safety of the trees.

In the end, a lot of snow had been thrown at them, and now all the family members were in their rooms, changing for dinner and holiday decorating time.

Lexie went to her room and changed, but she was still frozen when she came back out. She found Lance sitting in the same chair she'd performed her naughty-nurse act in, and she thought the heat flooding her stomach would warm her up, but she couldn't stop shaking.

"Give me ten minutes. Stand in front of the fire," Lance told her before he disappeared into the bathroom where she heard water running. Why she hadn't thought of taking a hot shower, she wasn't sure, but the fire wasn't taking the chill out of her bones.

When the bathroom door opened, she saw a soft glow coming from the room and wondered what was going on.

"Come here," he beckoned, and her curiosity wouldn't allow her to act like she didn't want to join him.

Stepping into the bathroom, she saw a tub of steaming water surrounded with lit candles. Her heart raced at the scene, and she thought of running away to protect her already weakened heart, but the heat coming off the tub wouldn't allow her to retreat.

Lance moved closer to her and was peeling away her clothes, and all she could do was look into his eyes as he smiled at her, stripped his own clothes off, and led her to the tub.

"Life is about simple pleasures," he told her as he helped her into the tub. She was so chilled the water felt scorching hot. It took her a full minute to sink into it, but when her shoulders were submerged a pleasured sigh escaped as she leaned back and closed her eyes.

"Oh, Lance, this is more than perfect," she told him.

He sat on the side of the tub, his foot brushing the inside of her thighs, and it was exactly what she'd needed.

"I want to take care of you," he said, his voice intense. Lexie was afraid to look at him, but she opened her eyes and glanced across the dim space, seeing the truth in his eyes. She wanted to tell him she wanted that, but she bit her lip to keep from saying it.

"I could get used to all this," she admitted, surprising herself.

"But you're afraid." It wasn't a question. "I just don't understand why," he added.

Lexie could keep it all in, not share anything with him, but she was so relaxed as the water heated her and the scent of the candles soothed her. Add in the feel of his foot rubbing against her leg and she had no willpower left to fight.

"My dad was a horrible man, like a *really* horrible man. It sort of ruined me on trusting people," she told him.

Lance was quiet a moment, processing what she'd said. She didn't want to look in his eyes to see if he was judging her. A lot of people had terrible upbringings, and they didn't use that excuse to run from commitment.

"You've seen your sister fall in love with a pretty amazing guy, so you know not everyone is like your father," he pointed out.

"Yeah, that's true. But I don't know what it is that I want out of life. I've always gone through the motions, taking forever to get through school, never staying in relationships very long, and avoiding anything that seemed too appealing, because if I convinced myself I didn't want something, it wouldn't hurt to lose it," she told him.

"We can go through life protecting ourselves, and we might not feel pain, but the negative is we also don't get to feel joy and love either. We would just exist instead of really living."

"I don't see what's so bad about that," Lexie told him. "I listen to love songs on the radio and so many are about heartbreak and trying to live again after it. Why would someone want to put themselves through that if they could avoid it?"

She really wanted to know the answer to that question. For many years she hadn't allowed herself to be hurt, but as she got older there was a different yearning that she couldn't erase.

"I used to think that way, Lex, but I don't anymore," he said.

"What made it all change for you?"

The intensity in his eyes grew as he sat up and moved closer to her. She inhaled a deep breath and couldn't let it out. That was a question she shouldn't have asked. She wasn't sure she was ready to hear his answer.

"I don't need to answer that," he said as he kissed her jaw. "I think you can figure it out for yourself."

Everything inside Lexie told her to turn away, to run far and fast from this man. But when he looked at her the way he was and touched her in the way only he could, she couldn't run from him. It would be like losing a piece of herself.

"Don't pull away from me, Lexie," he coerced.

"I'm right here," she whispered as his lips found that sensitive place on the side of her neck.

"I want all of you, Lexie, not just your body," he said, his voice more commanding. There was nothing cold on her anymore, especially when he reached between their bodies and ran his fingers along her aching core.

"Maybe you should take what I give you," she said before a moan escaped.

"Or maybe I will take it all."

He stopped speaking and connected their mouths together in a kiss. And Lexie stopped trying to fight what he was offering.

CHAPTER TWENTY-TWO

L EXIE LOOKED ACROSS the living room and a smile played on the corners of her mouth as she watched two of Lance's nephews tie him to a chair with tree garland. He was laughing as he promised the youngsters payback while pretending to struggle to get away. His three-year-old nephew was dancing around the chair, flexing his arm saying he had "mupples" and Lance would never be able to get away.

The other kids joined in, then Lance's brothers, with a gleam in their eyes, pulled out something a lot stronger to hold Lance to the chair before he was able to get away.

She was completely mesmerized and could picture the two of them doing the same thing with their own kids tying him up with the help of their cousins. It was a perfect family moment, and she wasn't sure she wanted to come back to reality for at least a few hours.

"I want the dirt right now, little sis."

Lexie jumped and wrenched her gaze away from Lance, focusing on her sister, who was stringing popcorn and cranberries on a long line to hang in the trees the next day.

For a woman who hadn't been the Martha Stewart type, she'd learned to adapt and now looked as if she should be wearing an apron and carrying a Betty Crocker spoon.

"What dirt?" Lexie asked. She peeked a glance at Lance who was now tied so tightly to the chair she wondered if he had circulation to his feet. He was a big boy, and she shouldn't worry about it though, she assured herself.

What was she supposed to be doing? Painting a pine cone. That was it! She returned her attention to the sadly spotty pinecone and decided it needed a lot more gold paint.

Her sister gave her a look that assured Lexie she wasn't going to get out of this conversation. Most of the family was in the room, but they were all working on their own projects, and thankfully no one was paying any attention to them. Still, Lexie hoped her sister had enough sense to keep her voice down.

"Do you realize how much you seek out Lance?" Savvy asked her.

"Shh," Lexie hissed as she looked around. Still no one turned to zone in on their conversation. "I don't do that."

"I love that you think no one else has noticed," Savvy said with a chuckle. "It's obvious the two of you are falling in love. I just want to know why in the heck you aren't talking to me about it."

"There's nothing to talk about," Lexie insisted. At least there wasn't when she didn't know how she felt, let alone how to verbalize it. And if she were going to do that, she wouldn't do it in the same room with Lance and all his family, no matter how big the room was.

"If that's the case, why are your cheeks giving you away?" Savvy asked with a knowing smile.

"Because I'm embarrassed that you're putting me on the spot like this," she said, giving up on her mangled ornament and grabbing a fresh pinecone. Maybe if she concentrated really hard she could do at least *one* right.

"Or you're having the time of your life and not sharing with your big sis, who has always protected and taken care of you," Savvy said with a pout.

Lexie could continue to deny there was much going on, but she knew it wouldn't do any good whatsoever, so she gave a long suffering sigh, set aside her ornament, and picked up her cup of eggnog, taking a long drink before looking at her sister again.

"I like him, okay?" she finally admitted.

"Oh, be still my heart," Savvy said as she leaned back with her hand on her chest, her eyes fluttering. "That was such a beautiful proclamation of love; I'm all aflutter."

"This conversation would go a lot further without the sarcasm," Lexie said with a grin.

"It might go easier, but it wouldn't be nearly as much fun," Savvy insisted.

"Why I tell you anything, I'll never know," she said, finishing off her eggnog. She had a feeling she was going to need a lot more to get through the rest of the evening.

"Because I'm the most awesome sister in the universe, and it's a crime you haven't shared more with me. When Lance told the family the two of you had fallen for each other and he was bringing you here for the holidays, I was ticked at first. Then I realized he was most likely doing it to stop the family from meddling in his life. But since you two have arrived, you've been nearly inseparable, so I think there's a lot more going on, and I think you're going to explode if you don't share it with your sister very soon."

Savvy pretty much had figured it all out. So much for Lexie being able to play poker. She obviously had a face that told the world exactly what she was holding in her hand.

"You're sort of right. He asked me to come and play his girlfriend, but then that kind of turned into a friend-with-benefits situation, and now I don't know," Lexie said. She desperately wanted to glance over at Lance again, but she refused to allow herself to do so.

"Why don't the two of you talk about it and see what's really going on?" Savvy asked.

It sounded so reasonable. But that wasn't going to happen, because Lexie was afraid of what he'd say. She wasn't sure if she was more afraid of him letting her go or wanting to keep her.

Before she was able to say anything more, she noticed movement out of the corner of her eye and turned to see a freshly untied Lance heading in her direction. Lexie turned and gave her sister a warning look before he stopped in front of the two of them.

"Need a refill?" he asked, looking at their empty glasses.

"That would be great," Lexie said. Both she and Savvy handed him their cups, and he moved across the room to the eggnog.

"Don't say a word," Lexie warned her sister.

"I promise not to if you promise to talk to me when we have some privacy," Savvy threatened.

Lexie glared at her sister, but Savvy wasn't backing down, and Lance would return within seconds. She would avoid being alone with her sister for the next few days, and then she wouldn't have to make a promise she wasn't planning on keeping.

"Deal," she said before Lance stepped back up to them.

"Here you are, ladies," he said, handing the cups over and sitting down next to Lexie, his thigh connecting with hers in the most appetizing way. She drank half her eggnog in one gulp. He raised his eyebrows at her but didn't say anything.

Savvy began a conversation about the kids getting the upper hand on Lance, and the tension eased in their small group. Lexie began to relax as much as she could.

Focusing on other people in the room and all the beautiful decorations and not on herself eased a lot of the stress. She managed to relax as Lance leaned back, his arm behind her on the couch, his fingers caressing her shoulder. She was growing so used to his touch that it now felt wrong when she didn't have it.

And for now she wasn't allowing herself to care.

CHAPTER TWENTY-THREE

S HOPPING TWO DAYS before Christmas hadn't been the best idea. The mall was crowded with brightly dressed people frantically browsing clothing racks and cleaning toys off the shelves.

But Lexie hadn't gotten her sister anything yet, let alone Lance, and she'd been left with no choice but to join Lance at the mall. She'd managed to get away from him for an hour while she'd searched for the perfect gift. It had been harder than she'd imagined.

What did you get for the guy who wasn't your boyfriend, but you were sleeping with, to whom you had no commitment, but whose family thought you were a couple? She'd settled on something, but she wasn't sure if he'd like it or not. She didn't have time to second guess herself before he'd found her and dragged her into a clothing department while he searched for ugly sweaters for his brothers.

Lexie had never understood the ugly sweater thing. Why anyone would want to wear hideous clothes was beyond her. Maybe the tradition started with someone who thought they were wearing a nice sweater that, to the rest of the world, looked like a train wreck. Whatever it was, the uglier the sweater, the better for those who participated.

"When is this ugly sweater party?" she asked as he picked out a lime green sweater with a sparkly tree and the most unattractive reindeer she'd ever witnessed on the front.

"Oh, this isn't for a party. This is a gift to my sibling," he said with glee.

"That's disturbing," she told him. She couldn't watch when the next one he pulled out was grey with multicolored animals on the front and back and "Hairy Christmas" written across the chest. "I need to find an outfit for dinner tomorrow. Take your time."

She went to the women's department and looked through rack after rack of clothing. Lexie wasn't a huge shopping fan on the best of days, but when she had to try to do it on the eve of Christmas Eve, it put her in a particularly bad mood.

"This."

The sound of Lance right behind her made Lexie drop the dress she'd been examining with a critical eye. She turned to tell him to quit sneaking up on her when she saw the beautiful red dress he was holding.

She examined it for a moment and decided it wasn't too bad, not something she would normally wear, but she was dining with billionaires for the holidays so she wanted to look like she fit in. She'd better not look at the price tag though, because she knew it wouldn't be cheap. She'd been searching the clearance racks. She was sure Lance didn't know what those looked like.

"Thanks. I'll try it on," she told him and took the dress, moving to the back of the store where the fitting rooms were.

A light was out in the back of the store with a ladder by it, but no one was around. It made the surprisingly unpopulated area of the store a bit spooky, and she was glad Lance had followed behind her.

"I'll be quick," she told him.

"I want to see you in it," he said.

"You will tomorrow night if I like it."

"Nope. I picked it. I get to see it today," he insisted.

"We'll see," she said with a sigh. She closed herself into a fitting room. Stripping down, she looked at herself in the mirror before holding the dress up to her. The color worked perfectly with her complexion. She undid the buttons on the back and slid it on, and sighed in pleasure at how soft the material was against her skin. She couldn't reach the buttons to do them back up, but even without buttoning it she was desperate to have the dress after seeing herself in the mirror.

It was a perfect fit, hugging her in ways she hadn't known a dress could and dipping low enough to feel sexy without going too far as to appear slutty. It stopped just above her knees, but it had a hidden slit that went halfway up her thigh if she twirled in a circle, which she did four times, making her smile.

She knew she should look at the price tag, but she was afraid to. Maybe she should just take the dress to the cashier, hand over her credit card, and ask the person to please not tell her how much she was wasting on a dress she'd only wear once. Wait! Heck with that, if she bought the dress, she was going to wear the thing every single holiday from here to eternity, including Halloween.

Sold. She was sold. Besides, it would be worth it to feel like she fit in with everyone else at the table. And she would be done trying on clothes. She'd rather order online and, if the item looked too awful, return it.

She was about to slip the dress off when there was a knock on the door. "Lexie, I know you have it on by now," came Lance's low voice through the doorway, making her knees shake just a bit.

"I like it. I'm getting it," she said.

"Nope. I want to see it," he told her. "Don't make me kick the door in."

Lexie was worried he might actually do that. The thought of causing a scene was so abhorrent that she lifted her shaking hand and unlocked the door, turning the knob.

"Okay, a quick look and then I need to change so we can go," she said as she thrust the door open and stood there, unwilling to go out onto the floor. Her back was exposed since she hadn't been able to finish buttoning the thing up.

His eyes flashed, looking at her from head to toe and then slowly going up again. He didn't say a word, but he didn't need to. She felt her body heat from his glance alone. Maybe the dress *was* too sexy, she worried.

Lance stepped forward, and she automatically stepped back until he was in the fitting room with her, shutting the door behind him. The space was too small for the two of them, and she felt her chest compress as she inhaled his intoxicating scent.

"What are you doing?" she whispered. "We're going to get in trouble."

"It's worth it," he told her in a low growl as he stunned her and dropped to his knees, his hands attaching to the outside of her thighs and moving upward beneath the material of the dress. "You turn me on so damn much."

Lexie was grateful for the wall behind her because at his words, she leaned back, unsure her legs were going to continue to hold her up. She had never had a man look at her the way Lance did, and it made her feel powerful, sexy, and desired. She wanted to continue to put that light in his eyes.

"We're in a store, Lance," she said, but there wasn't much protest in her tone. With him looking at her that way, she was willing to give him just about anything he wanted.

"Don't worry. You can bite into my shoulder to keep from screaming," he said as he lifted the front of the dress and buried his head beneath.

Lexie nearly fainted when his hot breath caressed the outside of her thin panties before he slid a finger beneath them and pulled, ripping the material away. She didn't have time to think, though, because his mouth quickly replaced his breath, and he was licking her hot core, and she was coming undone.

"Lance," she sighed as the pressure built within her. He didn't slow down as he pushed her thighs farther apart and slipped his fingers deep inside her.

"So wet . . . so hot," he groaned before he sucked her tender flesh inside his mouth and gently bit down.

Lexie bit her hand to keep from crying out as her orgasm overtook her, her body shattering beneath his touch. He continued licking her until the tremors faded, and only then did he stand.

"Yes, that's how I love your face to look," he said as he gently cupped her cheeks. Then he pushed her against the mirrored wall and lifted her leg while he undid his pants and pulled out his powerful erection.

Lance knelt and then surged upward, burying himself inside her before gripping her other leg and lifting her off the floor. She wrapped both legs around him and he slid the rest of the way into her. She leaned forward, pushed his shirt out of the way, and bit into his shoulder as he took her hard and fast against the wall.

She clenched around him with her second orgasm. At the same time, he groaned low in his throat and released deep within her. The two of them shook in each other's arms at the power of what they did to each other.

Lexie didn't release her legs for several moments as she held on tightly, not wanting to let this man go. But all good times must end. Slowly she untangled herself from his arms then felt empty when he pulled from her and set her down.

She looked in the mirror across from her and saw her messy hair and flushed cheeks, and she liked the dress even more. Lance stepped back and admired her as he fixed his pants and smiled.

Then he turned her around and pulled the dress off before carefully laying it over his arm. He pulled out a cloth napkin from his pocket and handed it to her, fidgeting a moment.

"Sorry about the panties," he said in a voice that didn't sound sorry at all.

"I just hope a bathroom is close by," she told him.

He pointed at the napkin and she looked at him in disgust. He just smiled even bigger.

"The dress is on me," he said as he began whistling and turned toward the door and began to open it.

"Lance," she hissed, grabbing her shirt and covering herself. He walked out and there wasn't anything she could do to stop him. She heard him whistling the entire time she threw on clothes and tried to fix her appearance so she wouldn't look like she'd just been screwed to within an inch of her life in a public dressing room.

But even after doing that, she was more than grateful to see no one was there when she walked out. By the time she caught up to Lance, he'd already paid for the dress and had it in a hanging bag that rested over his arm. She was going to argue, but that's when her sister and Ashton caught up to them.

Lexie kept her gaze on the floor and let the three of them talk. She feared they'd be able to read on her face exactly what had just happened if she so much as looked at them. But even though she was embarrassed beyond measure, she felt unbelievably good. Her current mortification didn't matter — it really had been worth it.

CHAPTER TWENTY-FOUR

IT WAS JUST a dinner. Lexie had to repeat that to herself several times. It was only a dinner, not a big deal. But the racing of her heart told her it was much more. She wasn't sure if it was because she was with these incredible people who also happened to have a hell of a lot of money, or if it was because she was dressed up and would be sitting beside Lance at this formal meal on a special night.

Whatever it was, she was a mess as she put the finishing touches on her makeup and then stood there, looking in the mirror. Maybe her nerves had to do with the fact that it was Christmas Eve. She only had two days left in this fantasyland she'd been living in for nearly a week. Truth be told, the fantasy had begun over a month ago when she'd first stepped onto that private jet and found Lance Storm joining her on the trip of a lifetime.

If she really thought about it, it had begun the moment she'd been visiting her sister on those docks she was working at and had run into Lance for the first time. When she'd met him she'd been tongue-tied and nervous. That had been completely unusual for her. She never ran from men. She flirted shamelessly and then walked away, not thinking of them again.

She hadn't been able to do that with Lance. At her sister's wedding, she had finally caved to her own desires and spent that spectacular night with him. She'd run away scared. This time she hadn't been able to run anywhere, and she wasn't sure she was capable of running anymore. She wondered what she would say if he were to tell her he wanted to be with her for real. That she was unsure told her how much she had changed during her time with Lance.

He wasn't in the room when she stepped from the bathroom, and she was grateful. For some reason, descending that massive staircase on his arm while they were both dressed up would seem more like a fairy tale. She was trying to come back to reality a minute at a time so it didn't all hit her at once on December twenty-sixth when she would return to what she was sure would feel like an empty home.

Lexie trailed her hand down the banister as she followed the sound of voices. She knew her way around the lodge now, but hearing the family in all their happy glory was comforting. She imagined the lodge would be spooky when no one was there.

Stepping through the doorway, her eyes caught the fashionably set table. A gold cloth ran down the center, with holly centerpieces and candles placed every three feet or so. Fine china plates and elegant crystal goblets were set in front of each upholstered chair. The silverware was shined to perfection, and it felt like she was stepping into a Christmas painting.

No one was sitting yet, and she followed the sound of their voices to the living room where she was stopped in her tracks. She'd been happy with her elegant red dress until she looked around the room.

The women wore gorgeous dresses, the men were in suits. But what really stood out to her were the jewels. She zoned in on her sister, who wore a diamond and emerald necklace that looked as if it cost more than most people's houses.

Lexie reached up and rubbed her earlobes where she wore her nicest pair of earrings. They had been a gift from Savvy when she'd graduated from college, a pair of half-carat diamonds that sparkled in the sun. Lexie didn't fit with this group. She wanted to turn around and run away but had decided after her sister had gotten her out of her parents' home she would never run again out of fear.

Sucking it up, she stepped forward and tried to act as if she belonged. She'd managed to do it many times before when she felt uncomfortable. She was glad she'd chosen the more expensive dress. If she'd shown up in a twenty-dollar clearance item she might have broken her rule and headed for the hills.

"That dress is putting very naughty images in my mind."

Lance's whispered words sent a shiver through her as his hot breath warmed her neck. He leaned down and kissed the back of it, and she felt goose bumps ignite her skin. She was afraid to turn and see how handsome he looked. But she did so anyway.

And her breath was stolen from her. The man looked good in nothing but a pair of sweats, or in a tight pair of jeans and a T-shirt, but in a dark suit with a red tie that matched her dress to perfection, he was absolutely lethal. She licked her lips as hunger stole through her.

"I have to say you and that suit are putting some pretty naughty images in my own head," she replied and smiled at him.

The hunger in his eyes made her forget about how insecure she'd been feeling moments before. This was Lance, who'd been nothing but good to her. She'd gotten to play out a fantasy without having to take any risks. She should be *thanking* him — she *would* be thanking him when dinner was over.

Lance circled around her as he looked at her from head to toe. There was a mischievous look in his eyes she'd already learned not to trust. She waited to see what he was up to.

"There's something missing," he said with a smile.

Lexie looked down and ran her hands over the back of her dress to make sure it wasn't caught in her stockings. That would have been mortifying.

"I don't think so," she said. She desperately wanted a mirror to double check.

"No. There is definitely something missing," he said again, then pulled a velvet case from behind his back.

Lexie's heart skipped a beat as she looked at the case. It was far too big to be a wedding ring — which she was relieved about. But she wasn't sure she wanted to know what was inside.

"What are you doing?" she asked.

"Here is your first Christmas gift," he told her, holding it out.

She took a step back. "No," she said, her voice barely above a whisper.

He stepped forward until the two of them were against a wall. "You can't say no," he said, that easy smile on his face.

Even if she wanted to take the case from him, her fingers were trembling too badly to do so. She shook her head. Lance's grin never left his face as he held the case and opened it.

Lexie couldn't help but look and then she couldn't tear her gaze away. It was a diamond necklace, a matching pair of dangling earrings, and a bracelet. They weren't small diamonds, and the chandelier light caught them, making an instant rainbow. The sparks that fired off them were enough to ground a plane. It was certainly in the same caliber of jewelry as the other women in the room were wearing, if not better.

She wrenched her gaze away from the stunning pieces and looked into his equally sparkling eyes. She shook her head again and opened her mouth. No sound came out, so she cleared her throat and tried again.

"I can't accept this, Lance. It's far too much," she said with tears in her voice.

He used his free hand and cupped her face in that way that made her feel loved and protected. She wanted to be alone with him, with no one around, so she could throw her arms around him and tell him it truly was the thought that counted. His generous gesture had made her feel so treasured.

"You can't not accept my gift. It would hurt my feelings," he told her. He set the case on the table beside them, cupped her other cheek, and leaned in to give her a gentle kiss. That small touch broke her, and a single tear slipped down her cheek.

He wiped it away with his thumb and turned her around. Lexie was too shocked to stop him when he wrapped the cold metal around her neck and clasped it in place. He turned her back around, raised her arm up, and attached the matching bracelet to her wrist.

He smiled at her. "I'm no good at earrings, so go to the bathroom and put these in. I will hold on to the beautiful pair you're already wearing," he told her as he opened her fist and placed the diamond earrings in her hand.

"I . . . I can't," she said again.

He continued to smile. "For me, please." Those words were her undoing.

"I'll just borrow them," she finally conceded.

He didn't argue with her, but there was a light in his eyes that seemed to say he was humoring her. He couldn't force her to take the jewelry. Walking like a zombie, she moved to the closest bathroom and shut the door. She was almost afraid to look in the mirror.

When she did, more tears shone in her eyes. Reaching up, her fingers danced over the sparkling diamonds around her neck. The jewelry was stunning. It took a couple tries to get her earrings out and insert the new ones he'd given her. As she scrutinized herself, she thought if she didn't know it was her, she might think she belonged with this wealthy family.

Her plan to pop her fantasy bubble a little at a time was completely thrown out the window. Lance had made that impossible for this night. She stayed in the bathroom until she pulled herself together, then opened the door and stepped out. She was determined to act like the confident woman in the mirror.

Stepping into the main hall, she didn't see Lance, but his brother Ashton spotted her and walked over.

"Would you like a drink?" he asked. He didn't look at the jewelry around her neck. She wondered if, at this level of wealth, the family was so used to fine things they didn't even notice them anymore. It was taking all she had not to reach up and assure herself it was still there. She felt the weight of it, but still . . .

"I would love one," she replied with a bit of a shaky voice. "Where's my sister?"

"She's nursing the baby. She'll be right back," he assured her. "Aunt Katherine had her favorite eggnog made tonight."

"Haven't we been drinking that all week?" she asked with a smile.

Ashton shook his head. "Oh no. Aunt Katherine only brings out her special recipe one night of the year, and you're in luck to be here," he said as he held out his arm. "Let me escort you to the table."

Lexie couldn't resist his easy charm. Her sister truly had married a gentleman. She laced her arm through his and walked to a beautifully set bar with eggnog and hors d'oeuvres. Ashton released her to accept a cup from one of the bartenders and Lexie perused the tidbits, choosing a piece of bread with melted cheese and herbs on it. At her first bite she was drooling. She hadn't had a single bad item since arriving at this lodge.

"Here you are," Ashton said.

Almost as if he had radar, his head turned, and Lexie followed his gaze, watching as her sister came into the room. Savvy looked stunning, her dark green dress flowed about her as she walked forward. She approached them and immediately kissed her husband.

"I'm yours for the rest of the night. The nanny has threatened to quit if I check on the baby one more time," Savvy said with a smile.

Lexie loved that many of the Anderson women had nannies to help them out, but they never left their children to be raised by them. They put their kids to bed, fixed their meals, and played with them. The nannies were there for moments like these when the adults were having a formal meal. But even then, the older kids were in the room with them, dressed just as nicely as the adults, growing to be as refined as their parents. It was amazing to see the multiple generations coming together.

"I will have to give her a bonus," Ashton said as he wrapped his arms around his wife and kissed her less chastely than Savvy had kissed him. She sighed against his touch, and Lexie cleared her throat.

Savvy pulled away and giggled. "Sorry, it's been rough with the baby to get a few minutes alone," she said, then her eyes zeroed in on Lexie's jewelry. As her sister smiled in delight, Lexie couldn't help but reach up and run her fingers over the necklace.

"Oh, Lance did very well indeed," Savvy said with no judgment.

"It's a bit much. I'm not keeping them," Lexie insisted.

"Of course you are. It's rude to return a gift," Savvy scolded her.

"But . . ."

"No buts. You thank the man for being thoughtful, and you graciously accept what he's given you," Savvy told her. "You would offend him if you didn't keep them. He would think he hadn't picked out a good enough present."

Lexie hadn't thought about that. But keeping them seemed wrong. And she would be paranoid having them in her apartment. What if someone broke in? She would have to get a safety deposit box just for the jewelry. Oh, that was all too complicated, and she didn't want to think about it.

"Thank you, Savvy. I was trying to tell her the same thing."

Lance joined them, and his arm immediately wrapped around Lexie. The nervousness she'd been feeling disappeared as she looked into his happy expression. He was much more relaxed than usual, and Lance was a pretty easy-going man on any normal day.

"You're having fun tonight," she said.

"It's a perfect evening. I'm with my family on Christmas Eve, and more importantly I'm with you," he said.

"I could get used to you saying things like that," she said.

"Good, because I plan on saying them a lot," he promised her, making her heart flutter.

"It's time for Christmas carols," Joseph announced. Lance leaned down and kissed her; Crew grabbed Lance's arm and dragged him to the piano where Katherine was sitting in her elegant gold gown, her white hair gleaming. Joseph stood beside her, looking every bit the proud husband.

The group all joined in for some fun versions of "Grandma Got Run Over by a Reindeer" and "Rudolph the Red Nosed Reindeer." Then Katherine began playing a sweet tune that had tears sparkling in Lexie's eyes when she recognized the song.

Joseph, George, and Richard began singing the lyrics to "The Friendly Beasts," their baritones blending perfectly as everyone hummed along.

Then Lucas sang the next verse, and another took over for each verse. Lance looked over to her as he sang the camel verse, and she was shocked at how beautiful he sounded. Katherine played for a few more moments and then Joseph and his brothers concluded the song;

Thus every beast remembering it well
In the stable dark was so proud to tell
Of the gifts that they gave Emmanuel
The gifts that they gave Emmanuel.

Lexie didn't even realize tears were streaming down her face until she sniffled and was handed a napkin. The group started another song, and she slipped to the corner as she pulled herself together.

"There's nothing quite like the Christmas spirit, is there?"

Lexie smiled up at Joseph, who moved surprisingly quietly for such a large man.

"No, nothing like it," she told him. "That was absolutely beautiful. Thank you so much for having me in your home this Christmas."

"You're a part of our family now, Lexie. I wouldn't have it any other way but to have you here," he told her as he patted her shoulder. He directed his eyes across the room to where Lance was laughing at something his sister Brielle said to him.

"My sister is pretty incredible, but this is her family," Lexie told him. She had to accept that her sister had found a new life, and she could continue to tag along with her, or she could make her own way. It was hard to break free when she didn't want to though.

"Lance is a good boy," Joseph pointed out.

"He truly is," she admitted.

"A woman could do a heck of a lot worse than him."

Lexie laughed. "Yes, a woman most certainly could. It seems the Andersons know how to produce incredible offspring," she told him.

"That's because we come from good stock," he assured her.

"How you've managed to build such a great family is a wonder. A lot of people in your position don't think about love above all. I've been humbled to be around all of you," Lexie told him.

"It's our pleasure to have you here as well," Joseph told her.

She knew he was simply being kind but his words warmed her heart in a way she didn't want to analyze too deeply. She was going to miss this rowdy bunch more than she cared to think about.

"Thank you, Joseph," she said. Lexie surprised herself when she reached out and hugged the giant of a man. Her arms weren't able to wrap all the way around him. He had to be in his seventies, and he was still as solid as his sons, but there was something so gentle and soft about him that she wished she would have had a father as wonderful as he was.

"Now you're going to make me cry right before dinner," Joseph said with a suspiciously tight voice as he squeezed her. Katherine called his name, and his eyes lit up as he released Lexie and went back to join his wife in singing "Silent Night."

Lexie wasn't alone long before Lance joined her. There was such softness in his expression that she wanted to grab a camera and capture the moment. This was what life was all about.

"May I escort you to dinner?" he asked her formally as he grinned.

"That would be most pleasurable," she said in her best impression of Scarlett O'Hara.

Lance linked their arms and took her to the dining room where the delicious aromas made her stomach rumble. It was loud enough for Lance to hear, but she wasn't offended when he laughed.

All the family came through the doors and Lexie again wished for her camera when everyone was seated, the setting too perfect to describe. Voices rang out until Joseph stood at the head of the table and looked around the group.

"We are so blessed to once again come together as a family," he said as he looked at each and every person at the table, including Lexie. Raising his glass, he smiled at his wife. "I'd like to begin dinner with a toast."

Lexie picked up her glass with the rest of the group, and her eyes met Lance's. Her glance told him everything she wasn't able to say out loud, and his smile faded as he seemed to understand. A look of what she thought was love replaced the easy-going nature he'd been displaying all night, and she wanted to climb into his lap and hold him tight.

Joseph began speaking again and the moment was lost — maybe forever. If that were true, it would certainly be for the best, she assured herself. She, along with the entire table, faced Joseph.

"I am thankful for each one of you, my brothers, my sons, my nephews and nieces, and my grandchildren, who continue to grow healthy and more beautiful, inside and out, each day," he said before pausing. "And as always, I am grateful for this beautiful woman who took a chance on me, who looked past my gruff exterior and saw a man who would love her more than life itself. I have only wanted the same for each of you," he said. His eyes stopped on Lance and then Lexie long enough that she squirmed in her seat and a few of the other family members chuckled.

"Merry Christmas," he finished.

"Merry Christmas," the group chorused.

Joseph sat down and the staff brought out their food. And Lexie fell the rest of the way in love with not only Lance, but with his entire family as well.

CHAPTER TWENTY-FIVE

DINNER WAS OVER and conversation floated all around them. Lance couldn't look away from Lexie for more than a minute at a time before his eyes were drawn back to her. She was different this night. Something about her made him think the two of them might have that future he'd been worrying about.

Maybe she had let go of the preconceived notion that all marriages were doomed to end in failure, or maybe his family had entered her heart like they did with so many. He wasn't sure what the change was, but the ring in his pocket was killing him as he felt it repeatedly through the night, wondering if he could do it, if he could risk rejection, asking her to be his forever.

His heart thudded at the thought of proposing. What would she say, or do? Would she walk away from him forever out of fear? Should he just ask her to make what they had official so there were no more question? That didn't sit well with him. He wanted her forever, not just for now.

Her sister said something to Lexie from across the table, and her lips turned up as beautiful laughter spilled out. Gorgeous. She was so damn beautiful his heart stalled in his chest just looking at her, hearing her voice, being next to her and able to touch her.

Unable to resist, he reached below the table and slid his hand from her knee, resting it on her thigh where her stocking ended. He played with the lace and she turned to look at him, hunger in her expression, before she leaned against him.

"Behave," she said, but then she reached over and ran her fingers up his thigh, and he nearly jumped out of his seat.

Maybe he shouldn't play a game of who could hold out longer while secretly touching. He had a feeling he would show his family a lot more than she would if he wasn't careful.

Lance glanced down the table and saw Uncle Joseph watching the two of them, and though Lance wasn't a man to be easily embarrassed, he suddenly had the urge to fidget in his seat. There was no way his uncle knew where his hand was, but with unbelievably youthful eyes, Lance was sure Joseph didn't miss anything. Lance picked up his wine glass and took a long swallow, breaking the connection of their look. But then Joseph spoke.

"Lance," the old man bellowed, and the other conversations halted as everyone turned to look at Joseph. Lance could practically feel heat coming off Lexie's cheeks as she looked at the empty plate in front of her. He had learned enough to know she hated being the center of attention.

"Yes, Uncle Joseph," Lance said casually, giving Lexie a reassuring squeeze on her thigh. Her fingers had stilled thankfully where they rested on his leg. He wasn't sure he could carry on a conversation with her rubbing him so close to his hardening body.

"I thought by now you'd be giving your family some special news," Joseph said. Lexie's cheeks heated more. There was no doubt what his uncle was talking about, but Lance decided it might be best to play stupid.

"I give you great news all the time," he said with a laugh, then turned toward his brother and gave him a pleading look to try to help him out. Crew only winked at him, and Lance decided he would pay the traitor back when the timing was perfect. He was definitely keeping score of how many times his siblings had betrayed him lately.

"You know what I'm talking about," Joseph said pointedly as he looked at Lexie. She didn't meet his uncle's eyes as she found sudden interest in her wine glass.

"Isn't it time for dessert?" Lance asked with a forced chuckle.

"I've noticed the beautiful jewelry you gave Lexie, but it seems to me the diamonds are in the wrong place," Joseph said as he grinned.

Lexie groaned as she tried to sink lower in her chair and disappear. Lance gave his uncle a warning look, which only made the man laugh as he continued giving Lance a look that demanded action.

"Joseph, don't you have more important things to worry about?" Lance pointed out.

"The wellbeing of my family is all that matters," Joseph said as he looked at his two brothers, and they nodded their heads, giving Lance the same look as his uncle. They were all traitors. And none of his siblings or cousins was helping him out.

"What is Grandpa talking about, Mom?" Jasmine asked. Lance wanted to warn the teenager to run and hide because her grandpa would be trying to get her married off before too long.

"You'll understand in a few years," Amy told her daughter.

Lance nearly laughed when Lucas gave his wife an incredulous look. "She won't understand for at least ten years," the protective father growled. That caused several chuckles around the table.

"Grandpa is talking about marriage and babies," Joseph said as he grinned at Jasmine.

Though Joseph loved all his family, there was a special bond between him and his oldest grandchild. From the moment he'd held her, she had owned him. When she smiled sweetly at her grandpa, the love in his eyes was clear to see.

"That's not so bad," Jasmine said before she looked at Lance. "Why are you so worried about that?"

Only an innocent child — even a teenager — wouldn't understand how much Joseph was putting Lance on the spot. But, of course he couldn't be upset with his niece.

"Your grandpa is meddling," Lance said with a smile to Jasmine.

"He says he doesn't meddle," Jasmine told Lance. "He says he just has to step up and help his stubborn family out."

"Well if that isn't a direct quote from the desk of the one and only Joseph Anderson, I don't know what is," Mark said with a laugh.

"My granddaughter understands me, that's all," Joseph assured the group. "And she appreciates her dear old grandfather."

"We all understand you, Joseph," Brielle said before she looked at her husband and winked.

"You know I don't have much time left on this earth," Joseph said, making his voice surprisingly quiet. The room suddenly hushed to where a pin could have been heard dropping.

"Is there something you aren't telling us?" Crew asked in shock. Though Lance and his siblings hadn't found their extended family until they were adults, they deeply loved Joseph and Katherine and their uncle George and Esther. They were as much family as Richard was.

"I'm old," Joseph said. "And I don't like wasting time." He punctuated this as he hit his palm against the table.

There were relieved sighs and then a few eye rolls. Joseph loved to pull out the age card when he was trying to get his way, but the man was healthy and would probably outlive them all. Why did they fall for his sick routine every single time? Probably because they feared that one of these times he'd be telling the truth. The thought of him no longer being around wasn't something easily swallowed. Joseph was larger than life, and he was the one to bring the family together.

"I should be upset with you, Uncle Joseph, because I had plans for a romantic night beneath the Christmas tree with only its light shining around us. I had plans to open a bottle of champagne and reminisce about good times together. I have played many scenarios in my head. But not once did this one come to mind," Lance said before he sent an apologetic glance to Lexie, who seemed confused.

Much to Lance's surprise, his palms were sweaty as he reached into his coat pocket and clutched the ring box that rested there before releasing it. He was going to do it, right then and there. He just wasn't sure he was going to get the words out that needed to be said.

"What in the world are you going off about?" Joseph grumbled.

But everyone went quiet when Lance stood up and turned Lexie's chair away from the table before he dropped down on one knee and reached for her hand. His eyes were for her only, unable to even think about his family members who were sitting around them and for once in their lives not saying a word.

"I have been planning the perfect moment to tell you how much you mean to me, to tell you that the thought of living without you creates a crater-sized hole in my chest. From the very first moment I stumbled upon you, and you gave me that sassy look that said you wouldn't give me the time of day, I've been chasing you. At first it was because you took my breath away, you were so gorgeous. But now I've gotten to know you. You're generous and kind, and you give the gift of your smile to every person you pass. You're afraid of marriage because you grew up with the worst possible example, but I'm here to tell you that you have no reason to be scared. Your heart is open and full of love, and I just pray that you will allow me inside, allow me to be the lucky man to win you. I love you, Lexie Mills; I love you with all my heart, and I don't want only one Christmas with you, or one trip. I want forever and that still won't be long enough."

Her eyes were wide as she gazed at him, and they gleamed with tears before spilling over and sliding down her cheeks. His own hand shook as he reached into his jacket and pulled out the velvet box that had been scorching him for days. Opening the box, he held it out to her, but her eyes never left his.

The two of them were caught in each other's gazes as they had a conversation for several moments without a single word being spoken. Someone passed Lexie a napkin, and she pressed it to her face, still without breaking eye contact.

"I didn't want to admit to myself how much I've fallen in love with you. I thought if I accepted this dream as a reality, I would somehow get lost and never be able to find my way back home," she said before she had to stop and take a few deep breaths. "But you make me so happy when I allow myself to let down the wall I've built around my heart. The thought of leaving in two days and never being with you again has been tearing me apart. I love you, too, Lance. I love you so much it scares me. It frightens me, the power you have over me," she told him.

He stood and pulled her into his arms, the ring forgotten for a moment. "I promise you, Lexie, that I will never take advantage of you or hurt you. I will mess up sometimes, and I will yell when I shouldn't, and then I will crawl on my hands and knees back to you and beg for forgiveness. I will get tired once in a while and forget to take out the garbage or forget a holiday. But I will never forget you, and I will never forget how I feel right here, right now. I will never give you a reason not to trust me," he said. He leaned back so he could look into her eyes. "I will be yours forever, and I will never abuse the honor of you accepting me."

Lexie shook in his arms as she gazed at him. And then her lips turned up in a watery smile as he saw the surety of how she felt about him.

"Then my answer is yes, Lance. Yes, a thousand times. I want to be your wife."

Lance's heart swelled to the point that he didn't know how it still fit in his chest. He had never in his life experienced such joy as hearing those words.

He grabbed the ring box and took her delicate hand in his before slipping on the ring. Yes, he would admit, the diamond was a bit big for her small hand, but he wanted the world to know she was taken, and people from rooftops could look down and see the sparkle on her hand, so he'd accomplished that.

His family cheered as they jumped up to congratulate them. Lance was ripped away from Lexie as the women hugged her and admired her ring. He was okay with that because he'd soon have her to himself, and now he knew he never had to be without her again. He could share her for a few minutes.

"Here you go, boy," Joseph said as he stepped up beside Lance and handed him an expensive cigar. "These only come out when you do something exactly right."

"I was getting there," Lance said.

"Sometimes we all need a little prodding," Joseph told him.

"Whatever are you going to do now, Joseph?" Lance asked with a gleam in his eyes.

"What do you mean?" Joseph asked, not liking the look when it was turned on him.

"Your last nephew has popped the question," Lance pointed out.

Joseph's eyes looked panicked for a minute, but he turned and looked at his teenager grandkids who were sitting back, thinking the adults were out of their minds.

"I don't have too long before they grow up," Joseph said with a sly grin.

Lance laughed and hoped Lucas hadn't just seen that look Joseph had sent his oldest daughter's way. If so, the old man might be in serious trouble.

Unable to stay away from his future bride any longer, Lance cut through the crowd and quickly wrapped his arms behind her legs and back and scooped her up. She laughed as she looked at him in surprised delight.

"What are you doing?" she asked as his family backed up.

"It's time we shake on our promise to each other," he said with evil delight.

"Oooh, I agree," she said.

Lance's body heated quickly, and he didn't bother saying goodnight to his family. It was time for him to be alone with his fiancée.

EPILOGUE

JOSEPH LOOKED ACROSS the living room, his heart swelling with so much love he wasn't sure how any man deserved all he had. The room was loud, and happy laughter could be heard from every corner as gifts were ripped open and children squealed in delight.

Yes, the presents were great, and yes, he enjoyed giving gifts, but the greatest gift of all was that they had each other, and, at night when they closed their eyes, there was someone beside each one of them who loved them unconditionally. That was what it was all about. That was why this holiday was so special to him.

It was unbelievable to think back almost twenty years earlier, to when he and George hadn't seen each other much, and he hadn't yet learned of his brother Richard's existence. So much had changed since then.

He'd gained three daughters-in-law, who he loved as much as his boys, and so many grandchildren. And now he had nieces and nephews, and great nieces and nephews, and his life was complete. Of course he had Katherine at his side, right where she would always be. He could lose every dime he'd ever earned, and he'd still be a rich man.

George was sitting beside Esther and had found not only one great love, but two. They still acted like children when they gazed in each other's eyes, and Joseph couldn't be happier for his brother. He looked over to Richard and felt a pinch of sadness that he hadn't found someone to live the rest of his days with. But there was plenty of time left, and Joseph had a feeling Richard wouldn't be without a bride at his side forever.

Lucas and Amy had been together for seventeen years. Time passed too quickly. They both looked so young still, much too young to be parents to a seventeen-year-old child. Jasmine would soon go to college, and then his son would feel that pinch as his home began to empty.

But Jasmine was the first of the next generation, and she and her cousins would bring so much joy to the family as they became adults and discovered the paths they wanted to take in life. Joseph looked forward to every stepping stone they'd travel.

Alex and Jessica had been through a lot, but their love had continued to grow, and Jessica and her sisters-in-law had a bond that couldn't be broken. Joseph felt blessed that all of his children lived close to home where he was able to be with them often.

Jacob wasn't far behind Jasmine in age, and he was a fine young man. He would make a great husband when the time came. Joseph could hardly wait to get his hands on the next generation. He knew his brothers were chomping at the bit as well.

Mark and Emily were the quietest of his children. They loved their life on the ranch and had open arms any time Joseph and Katherine came to stay with them. Out of all his kids, Mark was the most like Joseph's grandfather, and it always gave Joseph a pang to see similarities between his boy and the old man. It made him miss those easy days way back when.

Trenton was his oldest nephew, and he and his wife, Jennifer, were a true blessing to Joseph and Katherine. They were more than just family. They were friends, and there wasn't anything the two of them wouldn't do for the people they loved. Trenton had grown so much after meeting his bride, and had become the man his father had always known he would be. Joseph loved how Trenton would sneak kisses with his wife at every opportunity. The two of them often snuck off to be alone. That hadn't changed in the many years since they'd said their vows.

Max had fought getting married, but from the moment Cassandra had stepped into his life, the man had been a goner. She was his perfect equal, and the two of them still shared exciting adventures every chance they got.

His poor niece Bree had been the only female in the family for a long time. She'd been happy when her cousins and brothers had wed and brought women into her life. And Joseph couldn't be happier with her choice in a husband. Chad was strong enough to handle his spitfire wife and gentle enough to deserve her.

Austin and Kinsey had fallen in love while Joseph had been fighting for his life after he'd been foolish enough to drive a car too fast with his brother George at his side. When he'd seen how devastated his beautiful Katherine had been, he'd made a vow to never be so foolish again. He'd kept that promise to her, just as he'd always keep all of his promises. He didn't want to leave his wife or his children. There was too much to live for.

The day Joseph and George had found out about their brother Richard and his five wonderful children had been the day Joseph had known the blessings would keep coming in his life. He looked over at Crew who loved to travel to exotic places with his bride, Haley, but who also always came home. He couldn't imagine never knowing his nephew.

Joseph's only other niece, Brielle, had been a spoiled girl with a heart of gold. When her father had given her the ranch, Joseph had thought for sure there'd be more fighting. But from the moment she'd met Colt, all the fight had left her, and she'd been his as much as he was hers. And now they had so much more in each other than either of them had ever thought they'd find.

Tanner's inheritance had been that apartment complex that he'd refused to do anything with until their family friend, who happened to be a judge, had sentenced him to live there and play

Santa Clause at the mall. That had been entertaining for Joseph, George, and Richard to watch.

But of course Tanner had found love in his neighbor, Kyla, and community service was incredibly important to both of them now. When he'd been under house arrest, Tanner had threatened to disown the whole family. It wasn't until much later that he'd realized his blessings and had thanked his meddling family.

Ashton had been blessed to meet Savvy, and the two of them had fought their attraction, but in the end, fate was destined and all Joseph and his brothers had to do was give the kids a little push to find the way they were meant to go.

Finally, Joseph's eyes rested on his nephew Lance, who'd just proposed to Lexie. Joseph had known from the moment he'd heard about Lexie that he would be bringing her into the family. She was Savvy's little sister, and she was so filled with love. She'd just needed a safe place to be able to express it. He couldn't wait to see the children the two of them would make.

His family was truly complete now. All of his children were married, all of his nephews and nieces had spouses of their own, and so many children were running about he feared he might need a list in his office so he didn't forget anyone.

Joseph chuckled to himself. There truly would be no fear of that happening. He loved each and every one of them and appreciated their unique personalities and what they did for each other. They were family — in good times and bad.

"Ah, Katherine, our lives are so blessed," Joseph said as he grasped her hand.

"Yes, they are, darling," she said before leaning over and kissing his cheek. "But that is in spite of your meddling, not because of it," she pointed out.

"Like I've told you before, my beautiful bride, I don't know what you are talking about. I've never meddled in my life," he said, crossing his toes in his thick socks. It wasn't exactly a lie, he'd just prodded the kids along; he hadn't exactly meddled.

"And because I love you, I won't rant and rave," she said with a chuckle.

Fifty plus years of marriage and Joseph still had his breath taken away by the woman at his side. He gave her a sweet kiss before leaning back and smiling. They always forgave one another because there was nothing that could separate them.

The gifts were all opened and parents were sorting through the mess, making sure toys didn't get thrown out with the wrapping paper. Joseph sent a look to his brothers and they nodded, the three of them standing and sneaking off to the den where they had cigars and bourbon waiting for them.

They closed the door before Richard looked at Joseph and George with almost sad eyes.

"We've accomplished our goals. All the kids are married, or soon to be married. I don't know what we're going to do now," Richard said as he poured himself a double.

"I know, and my friends in Montana, and here in Seattle, have also married off their kids. We're running out of things to do," Joseph said with a sigh.

"The grandkids are getting older," George said with a smile.

"But that's still years away," Joseph told him.

"We do have our friend Walter Grayson in California who called the other day complaining about his ungrateful children," George said.

Both Richard and Joseph perked up. "I forgot all about that with all that's been going on," Joseph said.

"Maybe we need to go down and visit him," Richard suggested.

"I think that's a mighty fine idea," George said.

The three men clinked their glasses together as they toasted to love, happiness, and a blessed future.

If you've enjoyed all 12 books in the Anderson Series please also see the other places Joseph Anderson has managed to visit and bring chaos. Continue reading for an excerpt from "Turbulent Intentions."

PROLOGUE

TIRES SQUEALED AS a sleek, silver Jaguar shot out onto the highway. An unsuspecting car cruising along slammed on its brakes just in time to avoid a wreck with the Jag. The four brothers sitting in the Jaguar didn't give a damn about the commotion they were causing.

This wasn't unusual.

They continued speeding along, trying to outrun the demons chasing them as they flew down the highway, hitting over a hundred miles an hour and continuing on, faster and faster.

It wasn't quick enough. They kept on going until they hit the edge of town in Bay Harbor, Washington, where they found a dilapidated bar with a blinking neon sign that had some of the letters burned out.

Cooper, who was driving, jerked the steering wheel and came to an abrupt halt outside the run-down building. "Good enough," he said. His fists clenched with the urge to hit something, or better yet, someone.

"Yep," his brother replied from the backseat.

Getting out of the car, they made their way to the entrance, an undeniable swagger in their gait—a swagger that made people turn and watch them wherever they went. Though young, the Armstrong brothers already had a reputation in their small community for stirring up trouble.

When they entered a room, patrons would turn away, glancing back at them with a wary eye. The brothers were the first in for a fight and the last ones standing.

They were wealthy, and not above flashing their fat wallets, Rolex watches, and extravagant cars. They were also arrogant and hot-tempered, a foursome to both be leery of and look at with awe. Cooper was the oldest at twenty-four, each of his brothers one year, almost to the date, behind him: Nick at twenty-three, Maverick at twenty-two, and Ace, the baby, at twenty-one.

On this night, though, they were looking for more than just the usual trouble. They were out for blood, but the demon chasing them was relentless, and no matter how fast they moved, this was something they couldn't outrun.

Their father was dying.

Maybe it was the feeling of helplessness or maybe, for once, it was not being the strongest ones in a room. Whatever it was, Cooper, Nick, Maverick, and Ace were scared, and because they wouldn't admit that, they were trouble to anyone in their path.

This band of brothers had always been revered as much as they'd been feared. They were tall, lean, and had distinct green eyes that hid their innermost thoughts but shone with a sparkle that most couldn't resist.

Walking indoors, Cooper sighed in anticipation. Smoke filled the air as loud music echoed off the walls. A few heads turned in their direction, and Cooper scoped them out, looking for a potential boxing partner.

The nervous energy rising off him in waves needed an outlet, so the first person that gave him the slightest reason would feel the wrath of his heartbreak, denial, and feeling of helplessness.

As if the patrons knew this group was up to no good, they cast their eyes downward, particularly annoying Cooper in their weakness to accept the challenge radiating off his entire body.

The boys ordered beers, then leaned against the bar, facing out as they scanned the crowd. None of them spoke for several moments, each lost in thought.

Cooper was thinking they might just have to give up on this place and find a new location when his gaze captured the angry look of a man shooting pool. Cooper smirked at the guy and practically saw steam rise from the man's ears. The stranger began making his way toward them. Cooper's fists clenched with the need to punch.

"You're the Armstrong boys, right?"

The man was swaying as he stepped closer to them, his glazed-over eyes narrowed. Cooper stood at full attention. This just might be the huckleberry he'd been in search of.

"Yep," Coop said, not altering his stance at all.

"I hear your daddy's on his deathbed." The man said the cold words with glee.

Maybe the man was too drunk to know exactly what he was doing, but instantly the four brothers stepped a bit closer to one another, their knuckles cracking, their collective breath hissing out.

"Maybe you shouldn't listen to gossip," Maverick said in a low growl.

"Oh, I don't think it's gossip. You see, your daddy has run over many real workingmen to get to the top of that mountain he's built for himself. And now he's getting the early death he deserves."

Nick instantly stepped away from the bar, but Cooper shot his hand out and stopped him. "He was looking at me, Nick," he said, his tone deathly low.

His brothers shot him a look, but then they stepped back, letting Cooper deal with his demons, and the drunken bastard before them, at the same time.

"Dave, come on. You've had too much to drink," a woman said, placing her hand on his arm.

"Get the hell off of me. I know what I'm doing," Dave snarled at the woman, pushing her away.

Cooper's fingers twitched in anticipation. He wanted to deck this asshole even more now. It was okay to fight with a man, but to push a lady around was never acceptable.

"Maybe you should lay off the lady," Maverick said. He wanted to push forward and take Cooper's place. Cooper looked at him and Maverick stepped back, though it was costing him to do so.

"Maybe you should keep your damn mouth shut," Dave said to Mav.

"This is Cooper's fight," Nick reminded Maverick when he began to shake with the need to hit this piece of scum.

Dave turned away from Maverick, his beady eyes focused again on Cooper. "Are you just like your daddy, boy? Do you like living off the men busting their asses for your family in those crap factories?"

"At least our daddy provides trash like you a job," Cooper said.

"Not that you would know. You haven't worked a damn day in your life," Dave snapped.

"Nope. And I have a hell of a lot more than you, don't I?" Cooper taunted him, making sure the man could see the gold Rolex he was sporting.

The man spit as he tried to get words out. He was furious. When Cooper pulled out his wallet and slapped a hundred-dollar bill on the bar and told the waitress to take care of the man's tab since he probably couldn't, Dave's face turned beet-red with fury and embarrassment.

"I don't need the likes of you taking care of anything for me," he finally managed to sputter.

Finishing his beer in a long swallow, Cooper took his time before putting the glass down on the counter. The bar was strangely quiet as the patrons watched this scene unfold before them.

"So you're one of those guys who blames his lot in life on the big man in the top office instead of doing a day's hard work, huh?" Cooper said, a taunting smile on his lips.

"I like my damn life. I don't need some rich kid who doesn't know what work is telling me he's better than me," the man blustered.

"I *am* better than you," Coop told him with a wink he was sure would enrage the man. Just to add fuel to the fire, he pulled out a wad of cash and threw it at the man's feet. "Here's some spending money for you. Obviously you need the cash more than I do since I have a mountain of it back home."

"I'm going to enjoy kicking your ass, boy," Dave said, tossing his beer bottle behind him in his rage. Though he did look down at the cash longingly. Cooper would have laughed, if he had been capable of it at that moment.

His brothers didn't even flinch at the hundreds lying on the filthy floor, money that would be swallowed up the second the boys stepped away.

"I'd like to see you try," Cooper said with just enough of a mocking glow to his eyes to really infuriate the man. "Follow me."

His muscles were coiled and he was more than ready. He headed toward the door. He could do it in the bar or flatten this guy outside. Either way was good with him.

"You gonna leave the convoy behind, or do you need your brothers to save your ass?" the man taunted.

The fact that this piece of garbage was questioning his honor infuriated Cooper even more. He took a second before answering, not even turning around to face the drunkard.

"You obviously don't know me at all if you think I need any help kicking your flabby ass," Cooper told him. "Chicken ass," he then mumbled, knowing it would push this piece of trash over the limit.

The air stirred against his ears, alerting Cooper of the attack coming toward him. They'd barely made it out the front doors before the man swung, thinking that because Cooper was ahead of him he would get a cheap shot from behind.

He wasn't counting on Cooper's rage, or his soberness.

Spinning around, Coop threw all his weight behind a punishing blow that made brutal contact with the drunk's face. The resounding crack of Coop's knuckles breaking the man's nose echoed across the parking lot.

The man spit blood as he tried to get up before falling back to the ground. Cooper didn't give him a chance. In half a heartbeat, he was on the ground, slugging the man again and again.

"Should we stop this?" Maverick asked, leaning against the outside wall of the bar as patrons poured out to watch the fist-fight.

"Not a chance. Hell, I'm hoping someone else mouths off so I can get a punch or two thrown in," Nick mumbled, looking around.

"It's my turn next," Ace grumbled.

Maverick held his brother back. "You'll get your turn," Maverick promised him.

No one was paying the least attention to the other brothers as the fight in front of them continued on the ground and Dave got in a good punch to Cooper's face.

Within a couple minutes, though, the fight was over. Dave was knocked out on the ground, and with the show over, the patrons of the bar lost interest and went back inside to their cold beer and stale peanuts. The brothers watched as Cooper slowly stood while spitting out a stream of saliva and touching his swollen lip.

A couple of men picked up Dave and quietly hauled him away. The brothers didn't even bother watching them go.

"Should we go back in?" Maverick asked.

"Yeah. I'm done with this trash. Maybe there's another idiot inside looking for a reason to get a nose job," Cooper said.

Before Nick or Ace could respond, Nick's phone rang. He looked at the caller ID and sighed. It rang twice more before he answered.

He was silent for a moment as the caller spoke. Then he nodded, though the person couldn't see him. "Yes, Mom. We'll be there."

He hung up. "We have to go back home," Nick told them. Even without the call, Nick was always the voice of reason.

"I'm not ready to go back there," Ace said, his eyes downcast.

"I can't," Cooper admitted. He couldn't allow the adrenaline high to stop, because then . . . then, he might actually *feel* real pain instead of anger.

"It's time," Nick said again.

They didn't want to listen, but they knew their brother was right.

It was like a parade down the green mile as they moved back to the car and piled in. They drove much more slowly toward home than they'd driven away from it, taking their time, none of them speaking.

When they pulled up in front of the large mansion they'd grown up in, they remained in the Jag, none of them wanting to be the first to open their car door. Finally, though, Nick got out, and the others followed. Their passage into the mansion was quiet, their shoulders hunched.

"Where have you been?"

They stopped in the foyer as their uncle Sherman busted down the stairs glaring at them. The urgency in his voice had them terrified. They knew time was running out.

"We had to blow off some steam," Maverick said, his hands tucked into his pockets as he rocked back and forth on his heels.

"Your father's been asking for you," Sherman scolded. "And there isn't much time left. Your mother will need all of you."

"We're sorry," Cooper said. The others seemed incapable of speech and just nodded their apologies.

Sherman sighed, not one to stay angry for long.

They followed their uncle up the stairs. None of them wanted to walk through that bedroom door. But they did it. Their father, who had once been so strong, was frail and weak now, the cancer taking everything from him, leaving him a shadow of the man he'd always been.

"Come here," he said, his voice barely a whisper.

Slowly, the four boys surrounded the bed, facing the man they would soon lose.

"Time is running out so I can't mince words," their father started.

"Dad . . ." Cooper tried to interrupt, but his mother put her hand on his arm.

"Let him speak, son."

Her voice was so sad that the boys turned to look at her for a moment, their shoulders stiffening before they turned back to their father and waited.

"I've done wrong by all of you," he told them, disappointment on his face. He looked extra long at the blood on Cooper's eye and sadly shook his head. "All of you."

"No you haven't, Dad," Maverick insisted.

"Yes, I have. You're men now, but you have no plans for the future. I wanted to give you the world, but you've only learned how to take because you haven't learned how to earn anything. I know you'll grow into fine men. I have no doubt about it. But please don't hate me when I'm gone," he said before he began coughing.

"We would never hate you, Dad," Nick quickly said.

"You might for a while," their father told them. "But someday you will thank me. I'm doing what I've done because I love you."

"What are you saying?" Ace asked.

"You'll know soon, son," their father said.

"Dad . . ." Maverick began, but their father shut his eyes.

Cooper willed himself to say something, anything to break this awful silence. But he just stood there, anger, sadness, fear flowing through him.

And then it was too late.

Not a sound could be heard in the room when their father stopped breathing. For the last time in each of their lives, the boys shed a tear as they looked down at their deceased father.

Then Cooper turned and walked out. He didn't stop at the front door. He didn't stop at the end of the driveway. He kept moving, faster and faster until he was in a full-blown sprint with his gut and sides burning. He tried to outrun the fact that he was a disappointment, that he'd failed his father. What if the man was right? What if he never became half the man his father was? He ran faster.

Still, he wasn't able to outrun his father's last words of disappointment . . .

". . . And for my boys, I leave each of you, Cooper, Nick, Maverick, and Ace, a quarter of my assets, but there is a stipulation . . ."

It had only been a day since the funeral, and none of the boys wanted to be sitting in this uptight lawyer's office while he read a stupid will. It wasn't as if they didn't know what it was going to say anyway.

Their father, of course, had left his fortune to them; that is, what he hadn't already given them in their enormous trust funds, and to their mother and his brother, Uncle Sherman. They were the only living relatives—well, the only ones they knew about, at least. So this was a waste of all their time.

"Can you get on with this? I have things to do," Cooper snapped.

"You will learn some respect by the end of this," Sherman warned Coop.

"Yeah, I get it," Coop said. "Can I go now? I don't want to hear the rest."

"I think you do," their mother said.

Her sweet voice instantly calmed the boys. They did love their mother, had a great deal of respect for her, and listened when she spoke. But they had hardened through the years, taking for granted what had been given to them.

That was about to change.

"You won't receive a dime of your inheritance until you've proven that you will actually better not only your lives, but the lives of others."

Cooper spoke first. "What in the hell is that supposed to mean?" He was up on his feet, his chair flying backward with the momentum. His brothers were right behind him.

The world was suddenly spinning and none of them knew how to deal with this latest news.

"If you will shut up and listen, then you will hear the rest," Sherman told them.

The four young men were obviously upset, but slowly they resumed their seats, all of them except for Cooper, who stood there with his arms crossed, daggers coming from his eyes.

"You have ten years to turn your lives around. At the end of that ten years, if you haven't proven yourselves self-sufficient, by working hard, being respectful to your mother and your uncle, and bringing something to the society that you live in, then your inheritance will be donated to charity."

The attorney paused as if he were reluctant to read whatever else was coming next.

"Get on with it," Ace growled.

"Your mother and I shared a wonderful, beautiful, exciting life together. A man isn't meant to be alone. He's meant to love, to share, to grow with a woman who will help guide him through the hardest parts of his life," the attorney began.

"What in the world are you speaking about?" Maverick snapped.

"Son, this is in your father's own words, so I would pay attention," Uncle Sherman said, his tone sad.

Maverick leaned forward, but he didn't seem to be hearing anything that was being spoken at that moment.

"Shall I continue?" the attorney asked.

"Yeah, yeah," Cooper said with a wave of his hand.

"You will receive your full inheritance once you marry."

Dead silence greeted those words as the boys looked at one another, and then at their mother, who had a serene smile on her face.

Finally, Cooper was the one to speak again. "Mom? What in the hell is going on?"

She gave her son a sad smile. "Your father and I have watched the four of you lose your way these past several years. He knew he was dying and he'd run out of time to guide you, shape you. He didn't want to lose you forever, as I don't. So he changed the will."

The boys waited for her to go on, but she sat there silently.

"We're rich without his money," Nick pointed out.

She was quiet for several moments. "Yes, Nick, you are," she finally said.

"Are you going to take away what we already have?" Maverick asked.

"No, I'm not," Evelyn Armstrong told them all. "You don't have to get your inheritance, though it makes your trust funds look like pennies, as you know. But getting the money isn't the point," she said with a sigh.

"What is the point?" Cooper asked, trying desperately not to yell, but only because his mother was in the room.

"The point is to grow up. You need to grow up," Evelyn said as she looked each of the boys in the eyes before turning to Sherman.

"Your father wants you to be good men. He's asking you to show your mother that you are," Sherman added.

"So, even in death, Father wants us to jump through hoops?" Ace snapped.

"No, son, even in death your father wants you to grow into the men you are meant to be," Evelyn told them.

"I don't need his stupid money. I have plenty of it that he's already given me and besides that I have my own plans. If he thinks I'm such a screwup, then he can keep it all," Cooper thundered.

"Agreed," Nick snapped.

"I'm not doing anything because someone is trying to force it upon me," Maverick said, joining his brothers.

"If he thinks we're such screwups, he can go to hell," Ace said, pushing it a bit too far.

"Ace . . ." Coop whispered.

"Save it, Cooper. You're always trying to be the leader, but this is crap. Yeah, I'm the baby of the family, but that just means that I've had to try to make up for every mistake that you guys have already made. I'm done with it," Ace bellowed.

"Calm down, son," Sherman said, rising and resting a hand on Ace's shoulder.

"No!"

Ace yanked away from Sherman and then moved toward the door.

"I love you all no matter what you choose, but I hope you'll listen to your father's last words and know he does this because he loves you," Evelyn said quietly, stopping Ace for a moment. Then his eyes hardened.

"I'm out of here."

Ace was the first to leave. He rushed from the attorney's office, fury heating the very air around him.

Cooper stood there dumfounded. What was happening? They'd not only lost their father, but they'd all just found out that they had never been good enough in his eyes.

"To hell with Dad—and to hell with this place."

Cooper followed his brother, though Ace was already long gone. It didn't matter. Cooper would prove himself, but he'd do it because he wanted to. He would never be someone's puppet—not even his father's.

CHAPTER ONE

WHAT IN THE world was he doing at the lavish Anderson wedding of Crew Storm and his bride, Haley? He didn't want to be there, didn't want to be around anyone, actually, but he feared his friends were going to call in the National Guard at any minute if he didn't come out and at least pretend he was still somewhat normal.

It had only been six months since his father's passing. There'd been zero word from Ace, and though he talked to his other two brothers, the conversations were short. All of them were dealing with their demons and the final words of their father.

He hadn't spoken more than a few words to his mother, which he knew was terrible, but he couldn't see her while he was like this.

"It's really good to see you out, Coop."

Mark Anderson stood next to him as they scanned the merry crowd celebrating all around them. Cooper couldn't even try to smile. His lips just weren't turning up.

"I haven't felt much like celebrating lately," Cooper admitted to his friend.

"I understand that. I don't know how I would survive it if my dad died. The man's meddling and always in my face, but I love him. I think the old guy is too damn ornery to let go anyway. He's gonna outlive us all," Mark said with a chuckle.

"Yes, I agree with you. Joseph is a force to be reckoned with," Cooper said, his lips twitching the slightest bit. It was almost a smile.

"Are you enjoying your new job?" Mark asked.

Cooper paused as he thought about the question. He was doing exactly what his father had wanted, even if he was doing it in spite of his dad. He was working for a small airline, using the skill that had been nothing but a hobby for him up until recently.

"I don't know about enjoying the actual job and the paperwork that comes with it, but yes, flying is what I love. I can't seem to get enough of it. Who knew that playing with planes my whole life would turn into a career," Cooper said.

"Even without your inheritance, you're a very wealthy man, Cooper. It isn't as if you have to work. But before you say something, I know it isn't about a paycheck. I don't have to work myself. But choosing to work despite my fortune is a matter of pride," Mark told him.

"I didn't have much pride," Cooper said with a shrug. "Or at least I didn't think I did. Not until that reading of my father's will. I guess he was right in the sense that we have all sort of skated through life. But he raised us that way. I don't know what he expected."

"I think when people know their time is coming to a close, they start to get scared," Mark said. "Not that I would know from personal experience, but now that I'm a father, I get scared. I want my kids to grow into fine men and women. They work on the ranch, and they even go into the Anderson offices and are learning there."

"Aren't your kids really young?" Cooper asked.

"Yeah, but I was a bit spoiled myself. I don't want that for my kids," Mark told him.

"Well, I don't know what earning only a couple grand a month proves, but my father seemed to think that would make me a man, so now instead of flying for fun, I fly for an airline. It's not so bad. It just all pisses me off a little," Cooper said.

"The anger will eventually drain," Mark told him.

"I don't know . . ."

Cooper stopped talking as he scanned the crowd. Coming to the party had been a very bad idea. Maybe it was time for him to take his leave. He wasn't fit company to be around at the moment.

Just as his scan was almost finished, something caught his eye. He stopped and zeroed in on a woman in the corner, sitting by herself.

Mark continued to speak, but Cooper didn't hear what his friend was saying. He was too focused on the blonde woman in the tight red dress who was holding her drink close to her like it was a lifeline.

She nervously glanced around the room, not meeting his gaze, before she looked back down again. Cooper was shocked at the stirring he felt.

It had been a long time since he'd felt any emotion other than anger.

"Who is that?" he asked Mark, interrupting his friend mid-sentence.

Mark followed his gaze and looked at the woman for several moments.

"I have no idea. Haven't seen her before," Mark said. Then he smiled. "But I have a feeling you're about to find out."

"Don't overanalyze this, Mark. I'm just curious who she is," Cooper snapped.

"No judgments here," Mark assured him with a pat on the shoulder.

"I might like to screw the ladies, but I won't give my father the pleasure of marrying one," he said with a little growl.

"What does that mean?" Mark asked, looking a little lost.

"My father seemed to think a man's life isn't complete without a wife. I think all women search for a man with the deepest pockets," he said.

Mark gave him a sad look and shook his head. "Not all women are like that. I married a good one."

"Then you got the last," Cooper said with conviction. Then he walked away.

He didn't know why, but he had to meet this woman who was trying to hide away.

It was sex—that was all. And sex was worth throwing down a few dollars for, he thought with a cynical smile.

CHAPTER TWO

S TORMY HALIFAX WOULD have given anything for the ability to fade into the background. She tried in vain to squeeze herself back even farther into the corner as she watched the designer-clad couples swirling around on the dance floor, all of them laughing and completely at home surrounded by the glamour and glitz of the night.

Only American royalty like the Andersons could afford to pull off a wedding like this one. Stormy would bet her entire bank account, which actually wasn't that much, that she couldn't have afforded even a single flower among the many placed so elegantly in the hundreds of exquisitely designed centerpieces.

She eyed the door longingly. Just a few more hours . . . How had she ever let Lindsey convince her it was a good idea to crash the society wedding of the century? If Stormy made it through the evening undetected, she swore she would never listen to her best friend again.

Of course, how many times in her life had she had that same thought? Too many times to count.

At least she sort of looked like she fit in with the crowd—or somewhat fit in. That meant she looked *nothing* like herself on this beautiful summer night in Seattle.

Lindsey had insisted she wear the ridiculously tight red dress she currently felt plastered to her skin, and her friend had layered on so much makeup that Stormy felt like a clown. With the dyed blonde hair taking the place of her naturally brown hair, she barely recognized herself. When she had gotten a look at herself in one of the gilded mirrors hanging on the walls of the banquet hall, Stormy could hardly believe she was staring at her own reflection. The girl in the mirror almost looked like she belonged at the lavish wedding. Almost.

At least she looked old enough to drink. Even if she wouldn't be for a few more weeks. She reached up and clasped the chain around her neck, feeling more secure, if only slightly. She never left home without the simple piece of jewelry she'd designed herself.

Stormy scanned the room for Lindsey. Only the flies on the wall would know what excitement her friend was off having. Lindsey certainly wasn't hiding in a corner somewhere.

Enough was enough. With or without Lindsey, Stormy needed an exit strategy. She gathered up her glittering clutch, slipped her feet back into the ridiculously high stiletto heels she had borrowed from Lindsey, and then covertly tried to make her way to the door.

She was mere inches from freedom when she felt a solid, masculine hand touch her bare shoulder. Her breath caught in her throat and she froze. Busted. *Okay, play it cool, Stormy. Just smile, pretend like you belong here for five more seconds, and then make a run for it.*

"Are you lost?"

The deep baritone of the voice sent a shiver down her spine. She really wanted to turn and look at him, but at the same time she didn't. Cowardice wasn't normally one of her traits, but she was in uncharted territory and she was trying to flee.

"No. But thank you." She took another step.

"Are you refusing to have a conversation with me?"

Now she seemed rude. His voice didn't change, but she could swear there was a challenge in it. Dammit! Stormy couldn't resist a challenge.

Stormy finally turned, and when she looked up, she found herself gazing into a set of sea-green eyes with the longest eyelashes she'd ever witnessed on a man before. She found herself speechless.

"Let's dance," he said, holding out a hand, not concerned by her lack of vocal abilities.

This wasn't a good idea.

"I don't think so. I really need to go," she told him. But he didn't remove his outstretched hand, and she didn't want to pull away and call attention to them having this conversation.

What if the people standing around realized she was crashing this wedding? She was going to murder her best friend if she ever found her again.

"One dance won't take long." The deep timbre of his voice made her stomach stir. *Uh-oh.*

His dark hair was rumpled, and his stark white shirt, unbuttoned at the top, showed a nice view of his tanned chest. And those shoulders—oh, those shoulders—looked as if they could carry a roof trestle on them. There was a bit of youthfulness in his face, but he had to be a few years older than she was.

What was one dance going to hurt? The racing of her blood proved she wouldn't dislike it. Heck, even if she were caught, it might just be worth it to have this man's arms around her for a few minutes.

He said nothing else as he waited, confident she would cave. He was right. She watched a smile lift the corners of his mouth as he moved a little closer, and she knew she was a goner. His smell was wafting over her, a mixture of spice and leather. She almost giggled as the verse *Sugar and spice and everything nice* flitted through her frazzled brain cells. Wait! That was for girls, not for drool-worthy men.

"I guess one dance wouldn't hurt," she finally said.

The shiver that rushed through her had nothing to do with the warm evening air. She *wished* she could say it was chilly out.

Without saying anything more, the stranger leaned down and took her hand in his slightly work-roughened fingers. He pulled her toward him, casually wrapping his arm around her waist, his hand resting on her now trembling rib cage as he led her toward the overflowing dance floor. Without hesitation, he turned her, pulled her tightly against his hard body, and began swaying to the music.

She couldn't even concentrate on the song that was playing, he was holding her so close. Her heart was beating out of control. Wasn't this something she'd fantasized about many times on those lonely nights that she lay in bed after putting aside her favorite romance book?

She'd close her eyes and picture a handsome man finding her sitting alone somewhere. He'd have a smile that could light up a darkened room, but his gleaming eyes would look no farther than her.

As she began to relax and enjoy the moment, a woman's laughter made her tense all over again. Panic flooded her. What if this really was a dream—the dream she wanted to come true so bad? Maybe someone had even spiked that second glass of champagne she knew she should have turned down? This was too unbelievable to be real. After all, men like this man didn't dance with wallflowers like her.

As her arms rested around the back of his neck, she reached for her own hand and gave it a quick pinch. She knew she looked ridiculous, but she had to be sure this was real. The little jolt of pain drew a quiet squeak from her lips. Oh yes, she was awake. She didn't know whether to be elated or terrified by that fact.

"Is everything all right?" he asked, leaning back, those green eyes gazing into hers, just as she'd always imagined.

"Yes." The word was barely a whisper. Her cheeks flamed as he looked at her, a knowing gleam in his eyes. She was busted and she knew it, but there was nothing else she could do, so she continued to sway in his arms.

"I've been watching you for the past ten minutes. I couldn't keep my eyes off you," he told her.

Oh my! This man was either incredibly smooth, or she really had conjured up her dream man. Either way, she decided to enjoy this moment to its fullest. She found herself gazing at his lips as he spoke. He had beautiful lips—strong, firm, masculine, and turned up in the most appealing way.

"Thank you," she told him, feeling like a fool as she uttered the words.

"Are you here for the bride or the groom?" he asked.

The dreaded question should have panicked her, but she was almost in a trance now and couldn't help but answer honestly. "Neither. I snuck in with my friend. I can't find her now."

His eyes crinkled, though still, there was something restless about him that she couldn't quite interpret. Something was wrong, but before she could analyze that, the feel of him pressing against her wiped anything other than desire away from her thoughts. Stormy didn't have a clue who in the world she was right now. She certainly wasn't *this* woman dancing with *this* man.

She'd had sex once before, two years prior with her high school sweetheart. That had been a disaster and she'd never tried it again.

Dancing with this man was making her think maybe another try wouldn't be so bad. Did that make her an awful person? She didn't know.

When he stopped moving, she felt her throat close. She wasn't ready for him to release her. But he pulled back anyway, and where she'd felt his warmth down her entire front, she now felt cold. Then she noticed the music had stopped.

Maybe it was midnight and time for Cinderella to go home.

"Let's take a walk."

He began leading her away from the dance floor before she responded. His confidence was overwhelming her, but it didn't matter. There was no hesitation on her part as joy filled her. Later, she might ask herself why that was, but for now, she was in her dream world.

The sounds of the party began fading as they moved away from the tents and lights and then down a trail.

As he slowly walked next to her, with trees on either side of them and the moonlight barely filtering through, Stormy wondered if she should be afraid. As his hand caressed her lower back, though, all she felt was an overwhelming sense of desire and . . . *rightness*. Not knowing why it felt right didn't matter.

She soon found herself on a sandy beach, her shoes dangling from her fingers as she looked out at Puget Sound, the waves splashing gently against the shore. There was very little breeze and the full moon gave everything a soft light.

"This is incredible. I can't imagine being so lucky as to live here," she told the man. That's when she realized she didn't even know his name. Should she ask him? Or would that break their moment together? She sort of liked the mystery of it all.

"I think Joseph's place is a little too close to the hustle and bustle of Seattle. But I do love the Sound. It's a great waterway."

"Are you here very often?" Was she being nosy now?

"Yes. I don't live too far away." He stopped walking and she stood next to him, enjoying the clasp of his fingers in hers. "Sit with me."

He again didn't wait for a response, simply led her to a log and then sat down, pulling her to his side as they gazed out at the water. He put an arm around her and the feel of his hard muscles enveloping her gave her both a sense of peace and panic at the same time.

She tried to remember a time she'd ever felt so much agitation at just the mere touch of a man, but she couldn't think of a single moment. Only this man—only right now.

"I don't live far away either," she finally said, the silence too intimate. Should they exchange information? Was that what she wanted? Or what he wanted?

When he was silent for several moments, her brain spun. She began wondering if she was being a fool. This could be simply a case of a man trying to hook up at a wedding. It happened all the time, didn't it? Did she really want to be that girl the guys laughed about in the morning?

She realized she didn't actually care what gossip might spur from this.

Maybe she should be more worried. But how often in her life had she done something reckless? Not very often at all. What this man was stirring up inside of her she couldn't understand and didn't want to stop feeling.

"Where exactly are you from?" he asked.

The question helped slow her racing heart. "I've lived all over the world—in my youth, mostly third world kind of accommodations."

That had the man silent for a moment. Then he raised an eyebrow in curiosity.

"You can't just leave me like that. Go on," he told her.

"My mom and dad were missionaries until I was about ten, then they worked modest jobs after that," she began. "I was born in Portland, Oregon, but I lived abroad with my parents for half of my life, then in the Portland area after that. After I turned eighteen, I decided to move to Seattle."

"Now you have me curious of all the places you've been."

"Gosh, let me think," she said. "Africa, South America, Asia for a short time, and a few more places." Noticing she had his undivided attention bolstered her confidence and made her want to keep sharing. It was sort of nice.

"Of all the places you've lived, which one was your favorite?" His fingers were playing with her hair, making little flutters in her stomach.

"I can honestly say I've loved every place I've lived, save maybe a few apartments I've had in the city. But of all the places . . ." Stormy looked up at the starry sky to recall the fondness of a distant place in her memory. "I'd have to say it was Kosovo."

"Kosovo? Where exactly is that? In the Mediterranean somewhere, right?"

"No, it's not exactly in the Mediterranean, as it's landlocked on all sides, but it's right next door to Serbia, Montenegro, and Albania. It's a fantastic place. Incredibly dangerous at the time, but it was cool," she began. "I mean, one minute you'd be drinking Turkish coffee at a café and hear a car driving by playing Euro dance pop on the stereo, while the next car to pass would be blasting dance music in Arabic. The country was a collision of

Western and Eastern European culture, with distinct flavors from Turkey and the Middle East. Being a Westerner, of course, gave me instant celebrity status, which as a preteen, I didn't mind so much."

"That's always nice for a teen," he said as he pulled her even closer. The thing was, for Stormy, it felt right. Somehow she was connecting more with this stranger than any other person she'd ever been with before. "What do you do, Cinderella?"

She smiled at the name. Hadn't she been thinking about how this all felt like a dream, like she was going to disappear when the clock struck twelve? His words fit how she was feeling.

"My job isn't interesting," she hedged, and then she found herself playing with the locket hanging around her neck. "But I love to design jewelry," she admitted while her cheeks flamed the tiniest bit. Why had she told him that?

His fingers clasped the locket she'd been clutching as he moved to study it. "This is beautiful," he told her. "Did you make it?"

"Yes," she shyly admitted.

"You have a real talent," he told her, making her more nervous. Why did this man's opinion matter at all? It shouldn't. But somehow it did.

"It's just a silly dream of mine. It can't lead anywhere," she told him with a laugh.

He let go of the locket and gripped her chin, forcing her to look at him. She was voiceless as his gaze held hers captive.

"Dreams are meant to become reality. Don't ever think you can't do something just because it's difficult."

She knew there was a story behind his words. She desperately wanted to know what that story was. "I think it's time for you to share something about yourself," she said, very aware of how close his lips were to hers.

"No. I think we've talked enough for now," he said with a slow smile that melted her from the inside out.

Then she was moving. Effortlessly, he lifted her and sat her across his lap as he gazed down into her eyes. She was lost as his head slowly lowered, the moonlight glinting in his sparkling eyes.

"I'm going to kiss you," he said, waiting only a moment to give her a chance to say no.

Maybe she should refuse. After all, she didn't even know the guy's name. But she didn't want to refuse him or deny herself. She wanted to see if his kiss was going to be even better than his touch.

His head descended and then those exquisite lips of his were on hers, and she couldn't think anymore. The kiss was better than she could have ever expected. Her mouth opened to his, and he was caressing her in a way no one had ever done before. She felt the gentle touch of his tongue trace the edges of her lips before surging forward and commanding her mouth.

Shivers traveled through her frame as she rubbed her body against this man, trying to relieve the ache she didn't quite understand. When he pulled away, she leaned against him, not wanting the connection to end.

"My boat is right over there against the dock. Say the word and we can go and have . . . a drink or . . . something more."

His fingers were lightly trailing up and down her back and his eyes shone down at her clearly, the full moon making it seem more like dusk instead of closer to midnight.

This is where she should tell him *thank you, but no thank you*. Instead she felt herself nodding as she looked up at him. "I'd like . . . a drink," she said.

He hesitated a moment longer, and Stormy couldn't read the look in his eyes. But right then, she knew that she didn't want him to change his mind. Because if he continued walking her to the boat, she was going to do the first seriously reckless thing of her life—she was going to sleep with a stranger.

Then he smiled.

"Right this way." He stood with her still in his arms, and then he let her go so that her feet touched the sand. She hadn't realized she'd risen to her toes in an effort to taste even more of his kiss.

Excitement and a feeling of trepidation warred within her. But as her fingers remained tightly bound with his, the excitement won out. They made their way down a dock lined with several beautiful watercrafts. Her sexy mystery man led her to one of the boats and she stood before it and gasped.

"This is what you call a boat?" she asked, hesitating before stepping to the plank that led onto it.

"Yes." He seemed confused.

She suddenly giggled. Who in the world was this man?

"This is bigger than my place," she told him. If her night ended because he realized she wasn't one of the rich and famous, then so be it. She could only fake so much about herself and being impressed with the giant yacht in front of her was out of her control.

"Yeah, I got this several years ago. I guess it's a bit extreme," he said with a shrug as he shifted on his feet.

He wasn't running away from her yet. That was good.

The sleek yacht spanned at least a hundred feet, and it wasn't even the biggest at the massive docks. That's what was scary about this world of wealth she'd stumbled upon. But the part above the water appeared to have two floors. She didn't know what was below the water's line.

Finally, she allowed him to lead her on board, where she looked at the red hardwood floors and lush furniture. Once inside the cabin she couldn't even tell they were on a boat anymore, unless she concentrated on the gentle rocking motion she could barely feel.

"I didn't know boats had such large rooms," she said nervously as he led her to a living area.

He guided her to a comfortable chair and then stepped over to a big walnut bar with a giant mirror and shelves behind it.

"I don't like to feel closed in," he said before chuckling.

She had to wonder what he found so funny. But she wasn't going to ask.

"I noticed you with champagne earlier. I'll get you another," he told her.

In only moments, Green Eyes was sitting next to her, handing her a beautiful crystal champagne flute. She clutched its long stem and immediately took a swallow. She'd had a few glasses at the wedding reception, but the effects were wearing off, and she didn't want to chicken out on this once-in-a-lifetime adventure.

They sat together and she sipped her champagne, enjoying the quiet of the boat. Her eyes to roamed the yacht's opulent cabin and occasionally stole a glance at the man who'd brought her there. When she'd emptied her glass, he refilled it. She leaned back and smiled at him. She wasn't sure what to do next, so her lips were probably twitching a little.

"Maybe it's time we exchanged names," he said after the long silence.

She was feeling a nice buzz now and decided to play it bold. "I don't think so," she told him.

He turned his head to the side and his brow wrinkled. "Why not?"

"Because I'm enjoying the mystery of all this. I've never done anything like it before." She clutched her hands in her lap and twisted her fingers, but then forced herself to stop. She didn't want him to see how unsophisticated she truly was.

"Done what before?" he asked.

"Gone off with a man I've just met."

"There's nothing wrong with taking a walk or having a drink together." He scooted closer to her, his fingers rubbing along her bare knee. She was grateful she wasn't wearing stockings. She wanted nothing between his touch and her flesh.

"Ah, but that's not all we're going to do—is it, Green Eyes?" she said. *Damn.* Her cheeks instantly flushed after she threw those saucy words at him.

She was playing with fire, and she hoped to get burned.

"I hope not," he said after a moment's silence. And then he was smiling wider than the Cheshire Cat.

Stormy sensed the atmosphere change in the room, and she felt a little lightheaded as the sexual tension swirled around her. Green Eyes set down his glass, took the empty one from her fingers, and then stood up, pulling her straight into his arms.

This time he didn't hesitate when he kissed her—this time, it was fast and hard, and her knees gave out on her, but he was right there to catch her.

And she knew she'd made the right decision.

CHAPTER THREE

A S THE YACHT slowly rocked on the water, Cooper Armstrong looked over at the beautiful woman sleeping naked beside him—perfection on his bed. Just an hour before, they'd had the best sex of his entire life. That was certainly saying something since he hadn't exactly been a saint in his days.

His Cinderella had tried to insist on leaving right after, but it had already been four in the morning. He'd promised to get her a taxi at dawn. Yet, he was reconsidering her leaving so soon. He was even harder now than he'd been an hour ago and he wanted her again. He wasn't even sure one more time would be enough.

From the moment he'd spotted this woman at the wedding, he'd been feeling all sorts of emotions other than rage from his father's passing and the reading of the will. He wasn't quite ready to have her depart and let the good feeling end. Who was this woman? And more importantly, what was she doing to him?

From that very first glance into her somewhat terrified deep brown eyes and at the moue of her sensual pink lips, he'd had to walk over to her, had to see how she'd feel in his arms. Maybe the two of them would make love one more time, and then he'd be able to let her go. He didn't have time for a relationship, and he sure as hell didn't want one. Women couldn't be trusted—not when he had a bank account that made him more attractive in their eyes.

He knew he was a catch. It wasn't arrogance, it was fact. When a person had his looks, his wallet, and his ambition, it made him the perfect target. But the women of the world didn't know that he wasn't taking the bait. His goal was always to get what he wanted from a woman, give her the pleasure of his masterful bedroom skills, and then quickly slip away before the hook could slide into his flesh and snare him.

Even as he had this thought, he began running his hand lightly down his mystery woman's sleek body, the span of his fingers almost covering the width of her back.

She began to stir, but didn't quite wake, not even when he turned her so her luscious breasts were fully available to his touch. Running his finger over each one in turn, he smiled as they instantly hardened for him. She shifted, and he knew the best way to rouse her from her sleep.

He bent down and licked one nipple before sucking it into his mouth and gently clamping his teeth over it. She groaned, making his erection pulse painfully. As Cooper kissed his way back up to her neck, she reached for him, and he took her red lips with his. He could worship this woman's body night and day and still never have enough of her.

That was a sobering thought. And he didn't want to sober up—not yet.

When she trailed her hand down his abs and cupped his manhood, he lurched upward into a sitting position. He was so close to releasing right then and there. How had that happened?

"It's almost morning," he mumbled.

"Um . . . morning," she replied somewhat shyly.

"I know I promised you a taxi when you woke up, but I had another idea first," he told her, his fingers whispering along her skin.

She moaned again, and he was hopeful she would agree.

"I need a few minutes," she told him, and he nearly panicked as she sat up. He wasn't ready for this to end yet.

"Okay," he told her, and he was the one wanting to whimper when she climbed from his bed and walked into his bathroom.

He lay back on the bed and reached down to squeeze his erection, trying to lessen the infernal pulsing. It didn't help. When he heard the shower come on, he sat back up. Should he follow her or not?

When he couldn't stand it anymore, he jumped up from the bed, opened the bathroom door, and grinned as steam hit him full in the face. She obviously enjoyed very hot showers. But he could make it even hotter.

The mirror had already fogged up, and when he drew the curtain aside, the sight of this woman, with water glistening off her body, had him dripping in excitement. He just stood there for a moment as she rubbed her slim fingers down her breasts, across the flat plane of her stomach, and dipped into the folds of her womanhood while cleaning herself.

Enough of this watching!

Cooper stepped inside the shower with her, and when she opened those dark eyes of hers, which were already filled with wanton delight, he nearly fell to his knees.

"You are so damn sexy," he groaned, pushing her back against the coolness of the tile wall and making her gasp.

"Only with you," she admitted.

That knowledge was the most intense aphrodisiac ever. He moved his hands oh so slowly from her hips, up her sides, and around the edges of her breasts. His magic fingers came close to her swollen nipples, but not close enough. She groaned her displeasure at the way he was teasing her.

After looking into her expressive eyes, he finally let his thumbs glance over those hard peaks before sliding his hands to her stomach and circling them behind her to squeeze the cheeks of her firm ass.

"Kiss me," she said, and she reached behind his head and pulled him to her.

He was more than happy to oblige.

Running his tongue over her lips, he quickly parted them and thrust inside, in just the way he wanted to thrust into her heat. She drew him more tightly to her and returned his kiss with the same intense passion.

A cry of pleasure escaped her beautiful lips when he slid a hand back around and rubbed his fingers against her wet heat, and then pinched her little bundle of nerves, making her shake.

"I need to taste you," he said, after ripping his mouth away from her lips. He licked his way down her chest and dropped to his knees.

Gripping her thighs, he pushed them apart and looked up at her smooth perfection, her sweet folds gleaming with water and pleasure. He ran his hand up and didn't stop until he'd buried two fingers deep within her.

Only then did he lean forward to suck the most sensitive part of her into his mouth, flicking his tongue repeatedly against it as his fingers found a perfect rhythm of pumping in and out of her.

His midnight woman clutched his head tightly, and her cries told him she was coming closer and closer to release. Yes, he wanted to give her pleasure—over and over and over again.

So he didn't stop pleasing her with his fingers and tongue until she screamed and almost crumpled right there in front of him.

Cooper stood up quickly, more than ready to be inside this woman. Bracing his foot on the tiled shower bench, he lifted one of her legs and draped it over his so his hardness was poised at her entrance, her thighs spread wide. He gripped himself and rubbed his arousal along the open seam of her pink core.

"Ohh, that's so good. Please . . . more," she moaned, leaning her head against the shower wall.

Moving his manhood up and down over her swollen nub a few times more, he waited until he was coated in her juices, then he poised himself for entry.

"Open your eyes," he commanded her.

She opened them just a little, and, after pulling her up, he slid all the way inside her tight heat.

Her mouth opened in a gasp and he took the opportunity to thrust his tongue inside in perfect rhythm with the way he was plunging into her body, all while gripping her delectable derrière.

The sound of their wet bodies slapping against each other was driving Cooper wild. He sped up and almost poured his seed into her when she tightened around him again. She gave another long and impassioned cry.

He stopped thrusting and held her as she shuddered in ecstasy, and he gently caressed her mouth and squeezed her buttocks. When she slumped against him again, he pulled from her. An act of amazing willpower.

"I'm so worn out," she said, leaning her head against his shoulder.

"It's not over, beautiful, not yet," he whispered into her ear.

"I can't do any more," she told him.

"Oh, yes, yes, you can," he assured her.

Her eyes flew up, and he smiled at her before he turned her around and pressed his arousal against the exquisite cushion of her ass.

"Grip the edge of the bench," he told her as he pushed against her upper back.

She leaned down, leaving her derrière up in the air. Dropping to his knees, he bit each of those cheeks in turn before soothing the red spots with his tongue, and then he stood again and rested his pulsing erection in the valley she was presenting to him, enjoying how perfect the deep red looked against her light skin.

With his foot, he pushed her legs apart—wider—wider—even wider. When she was fully opened up to him, he reached around and found her still-swollen nub, which he stroked a few times, making her twitch against him.

With his other hand he guided himself down the middle of her ass until he reached her core, and then he thrust back inside her. Now it was time for them both to feel pleasure.

She groaned as he moved his hand between her folds, up her belly to her tender nipples, and then back again. He continued caressing her with one hand while gripping her hip with the other, thrusting and thrusting.

"Come for me one more time, baby," he told her as he felt his release drawing nearer.

He flicked his fingers against her bud and she screamed as she convulsed around him so intensely that he almost reached orgasm without any movement at all. But he had to move. Pushing deep inside her, he released a hot stream of pleasure, pulsing over and over again until he was entirely drained.

When he could finally take a step back, Cooper felt lost pulling away from her heat. And she nearly collapsed before him, but he was able to catch her.

"That was . . . it was . . . I don't even know how . . ." She was clearly at a loss for words.

"It was perfect," he told her as he lifted her in his arms and then stepped from the shower. He grabbed a couple of towels before carrying her back to his room.

He dried her off before laying her down gently on the bed, and he quickly dried himself. Then he joined her, pulling her back into his arms. He wasn't willing to let her go just yet. Or anytime soon, for that matter.

He'd be careful, he assured himself. This was only sex—just really, really good sex. The thought didn't appease him like it should have as he finally closed his eyes and fell into an exhausted slumber.

CHAPTER FOUR

NEVER BEFORE HAD Stormy had to do the walk of shame, but as she grabbed her tiny handbag and slowly crept away from Green Eyes' bedroom, she glanced back over her shoulder and took in a deep breath.

Dang, the man was good-looking—beyond good-looking, actually, especially now, with stubble on his strong jawline and his muscled arm thrown up above his head, the blankets resting very low on his beautiful hips. Just a few more inches . . .

No, she didn't need to entertain that thought. This was a man she would never see again. Their only connection was the Anderson wedding—a wedding she'd crashed. Her one night of debauchery couldn't cause any repercussions.

When she was on the upper deck of his boat, she peeked out to see whether anyone was around. How paranoid was that? It was about eight in the morning and the wedding reception had gone on long into the night. Everyone was most likely asleep and cruising for a champagne bruising.

Still, she was going to have to trek back up the trail they'd come down the night before, sneak out to the front gate—which had seemed to be a mile from the Anderson castle—and then pray that it was open. The last thing she wanted to do was trudge back to the house and beg someone to let her out.

They'd know exactly what she'd been doing. And even though they had no idea who she was and she would never see them again, her embarrassment would be incalculable. She knew it shouldn't matter, but she cared about what people thought of her.

Stormy made it to the top of the trail and then peered out at the house, surprised to see activity in the backyard. Trucks were there hauling things away and the yard was almost back to normal, or what she assumed was normal, after that enormous party. Wow! These Anderson people moved really fast.

Putting her head down, she walked as quickly as her body-hugging little red dress would allow. She made no eye contact with anyone as she hurried along.

"Hello there!"

The boisterous voice startled her so much, she dropped her purse and jumped into the air. As she came back down, off balance, the heel on her shoe snapped, and after wobbling for a moment, she landed hard on her rear end.

"I'm so sorry, darling," the man said—a freaking giant.

He approached quickly, moving far faster than she would think a man his age could. Bending down, he reached for her hand and easily tugged her back to her feet, where she teetered on the broken shoe.

She had no doubt that this was the famous Joseph Anderson, and she fully understood his reputation as a man to whom no one could ever say no.

"Don't worry about it. I was in my own world," she said, looking way up at his concerned expression. He had to be many,many inches over six feet. She only stood five feet six—in heels, and she was now short one of those. His silver hair only made him more distinguished in her opinion, and the twinkle in his surprisingly sharp blue eyes made her instantly inclined to trust him.

"Come on inside and we'll get you fixed up," he insisted as he pulled her toward the house. She stumbled behind him.

Uh-oh, maybe she could imagine telling him no after all. She wasn't going into his house. Not a chance. She had to get away before Green Eyes awoke.

"Oh, no. I was just getting ready to leave," she said, trying without success to tug against the beast of a man.

"I can't send you off without making sure you're all right, not after causing you to fall," Joseph said.

"I promise you, I'm okay. I really just want to get going now," she said as she continued to stumble along after him.

He stopped and looked at her, and Stormy's cheeks flushed at what he must be thinking. He had to know she'd just walked away from someone's bed. He must be wondering which guy it had been. Maybe he was worried about it being one of his kin. For all she knew, Green Eyes was related to Joseph. The man had sported a really nice boat that was docked on the Anderson pier.

"I'm Joseph Anderson, by the way," he said, releasing his protective grip on her hand. It seemed as though he expected her to now introduce herself. Something she absolutely didn't want to do.

"It's very nice to meet you, Mr. Anderson. As I said, I'm doing just fine, so I'll be on my way," she said as she retreated. The first thing she did was remove her shoes and grip them tightly in one hand.

"Where's your car parked, Miss . . . ?" He trailed off, obviously waiting for her to give her name again.

"I rode here with a friend. I've called a cab, and it's picking me up at the gate, so I'd best hurry," she said. She hadn't yet called the damned cab, but she was planning to as soon as she escaped from the intimidating Anderson patriarch.

"Then I'll walk you to the gate," Joseph said.

This walk of shame just kept on getting worse and worse. Now the man was going to catch her in a lie. Her humiliation was complete.

"Well, I haven't actually called the cab yet. I was just getting ready to when I ran into you. So I had best get going and do that.

By the time I get to the gate, the cab will be waiting for me," she said with a sheepish laugh.

"Nonsense, young lady. If you were a guest at the party, I insist on having my driver give you a ride home," Joseph said, once again tugging on her arm.

Stormy gasped. "I couldn't have you do that."

"I won't take no for an answer."

And that was why the man always got his way, she decided.

Within a minute, a black car pulled up; a man emerged from the driver's side and opened the back door for her. Stormy found herself practically pushed into the car, and the only relief she felt was when the car pulled away from the Anderson mansion.

She didn't look back to see Joseph reach down and pick up the locket that had dropped from her neck, or the smile he wore as he held it.

All fairy tales must come to an end, and when she got home and walked inside, she was cruelly thrust back into the real world—her carriage was now a pumpkin again, and her glass slipper left behind . . .

Turbulent Intentions is now available!